Love is
a time of enchantment:
in it all days are fair and all fields
green. Youth is blest by it,
old age made benign: the eyes of love see
roses blooming in December,
and sunshine through rain. Verily
is the time of true-love
a time of enchantment — and
Oh! how eager is woman
to be bewitched!

This item
latest
period

RUNAWAY HILL

When the dashing Sir Randal Thornton
aids Drusilla during the Parliamentary
siege of Reading, she realises how
foolish she is to fall in love with
him. Especially since her brother is
fighting for Parliament, and was one of
the deputation which protested about
the King's Ship Money tax. But having
glimpsed the possibility of happiness,
she is even more determined to marry
for love.

Books by Marina Oliver
in the Ulverscroft Large Print Series:

HIGHLAND DESTINY
CAVALIER COURTSHIP

MARINA OLIVER

RUNAWAY HILL

Complete and Unabridged

ULVERSCROFT
Leicester

First published in Great Britain in 1981 by
Robert Hale Limited
London

First Large Print Edition
published February 1992

British Library CIP Data

Oliver, Marina *1934* –
Runaway Hill. — Large print ed. —
Ulverscroft large print series: romance
I. Title
823.914 [F]

ISBN 0–7089–2592–8

Published by
F. A. Thorpe (Publishing) Ltd.
Anstey, Leicestershire
Set by Words & Graphics Ltd.
Anstey, Leicestershire
Printed and bound in Great Britain by
T. J. Press (Padstow) Ltd., Padstow, Cornwall

1

"**M**ASTER BLAGRAVE has called, Ma'am," the young maid Meg announced, casting a speculative glance at her mistress's young sister-in-law, who sat dutifully embroidering a seat cover beside the fire. Drusilla Matthews did not disappoint Meg's expectations, for she looked up quickly, abandoning her needle, and began to speak hurriedly. Elizabeth smilingly shook her head, and as Drusilla subsided, pressing her rosy lips firmly together, and veiling her large brown eyes with a fringe of dark, thick, curling lashes, Mistress Matthews calmly bade Meg to show the gentleman in.

"Why could you not deny him?" Drusilla burst out, as Meg closed the door behind her, and rose impetuously to her feet to pace quickly up and down the parlour where they sat, her dark curls bouncing against the spotless white collar fringed with lace that brightened her otherwise demure grey gown.

"It would be futile, my dear, as well as impolite, for you may be sure he knows full well that we are at home. And pray take care what you say before Meg, for her besetting fault is gossip, and one of her sisters works in Mistress Blagrave's house."

"Then the sooner my opinion of him reaches that house the better!" Drusilla snapped pettishly. "Then we might be spared these importunate visits!"

There was no time for more, since Meg reappeared, conducting a young man into the room. She lingered hopefully, watching to see what reception he found, but a frown from her mistress as Elizabeth rose to greet the visitor sent her swiftly from the room.

Mr Blagrave was a man in his mid-twenties, tall and broadly built, with powerful muscles, but showing already the effects of a wealthy background and good living in a highly coloured complexion and a tendency to corpulence. He bowed to Elizabeth, and responded politely to her greetings, then turned to look hungrily at Drusilla, who had moved across to the window and appeared to be dividing her attention between him and something of absorbing interest in the street outside.

"Mistress Drusilla," he breathed softly, and as he bowed to kiss her hand Drusilla cast an imploring look across at Elizabeth, who smiled brightly at her and begged Mr Blagrave to tell her how the members of his family did.

"They could scarce have developed plague and smallpox since yesterday," Drusilla muttered angrily to herself, and plumped down on to the settle again, seizing her needlework and affecting an absorption in it which she rarely showed.

Mr Blagrave replied punctiliously to Elizabeth's polite queries, but with considerably less embellishment than usual, and it was soon clear to both ladies that he was big with news. Having satisfied the proprieties and asked after both their healths, he turned portentously to Elizabeth.

"The fighting has begun!" he announced, with what Drusilla considered unnecessary relish. The news, however, was of sufficient interest to cause her to drop her needle and demand to be told more.

"The King has thrown down the gauntlet! News has just reached Reading that he attacked Parliament's army near Warwick, at a place called Edge Hill."

"What happened? Who won?" Drusilla asked urgently.

"You need not be afraid, Mistress Drusilla," he said soothingly, and she fumed inwardly at his tone. "My Lord Essex has halted the King's army easily enough. Why, you would not expect a rabble of soft courtiers and foreign adventurers to prevail over the might of Parliament, would you?" he laughed.

"So the King has been defeated?" Elizabeth interposed swiftly. "What will happen now, do you think?"

"Doubtless he will try to regroup his forces in the north, and possibly make another attempt to reach London. But it will avail him nought, and the sooner he realises it and negotiates the matter sensibly with Parliament, the better for us all."

"The King was not captured, then?"

"No, but I have heard few details as yet. I hurried to apprise you of the news the moment I heard it, for doubtless you are anxious, Mistress Matthews, with your husband away in London."

"What details have you?" Elizabeth asked.

"Simply that the King was marching towards London, and Lord Essex had been sent to stop him. The two armies met at this place between Warwick and Banbury, and fought all day, with many men being killed. The Earl had the better of the fighting, and the Royalists were glad to withdraw by nightfall. They will surely be licking their wounds for weeks to come."

"So James will be home shortly, mayhap," Elizabeth said, a smile playing on her lips.

"Undoubtedly," Mr Blagrave assured her. "Have you heard from him of late?"

"He sent me a message a week since. The deputation has been received by Parliament, and he expects to return soon. He opines that our grievances will be redressed now."

"Indeed I trust so! It was iniquitous to demand Ship Money from the people of Reading! What have we to do with ships! We submitted and paid over five hundred pounds in '35 and '36, and the King demanded yet more! It is good that the Mayor and Corporation have seen fit to deny those further demands, or there would soon be no free Englishmen left!"

"But what will happen to the King?" Drusilla asked, uninterested in the complexities of the Ship Tax.

"Eventually he must come to terms with his Parliament and agree to their just demands. Parliament have appointed a new Governor for the town, had you heard?"

"No, for you are first to bring us all the news," Drusilla replied tartly. "Who is it?"

"Colonel Henry Marten. He is the man that tore up the King's commission of array at Longworth, and then raised a regiment of horse. A worthy man, though I am told he has too ready an eye for a pretty girl," he added, throwing Drusilla an arch look. "You will certainly meet with his favour, Mistress Drusilla!"

Drusilla vouchsafed no reply apart from a darkling glance, and Mr Blagrave chuckled smugly. To her relief he soon took his leave, saying that he ought to return home to dispel any fears his mother might be entertaining if she heard any wild rumours of the fighting.

"Oh, he is abominable!" she exclaimed almost before the door was closed behind him, and Elizabeth quickly hushed her.

"He might hear, Dru!"

"Mayhap it would be to our advantage, for then we might be spared his visits!"

"Why have you taken him in such aversion?"

"How can anyone not dislike him! He is so pompous, and self-opinionated! He is for ever condescending to explain to me perfectly simple matters that I understand as well as he!"

"I grant that he is a serious young man, but that is no fault! I suspect he is over-anxious to please, for you must see that he is greatly taken with you."

"Unfortunately! And as hints do not suffice to discourage him I shall be forced to be plainer to him if he does not cease these unwelcome attentions."

"I pray you will not be discourteous, my dear," Elizabeth pleaded in some alarm, for she knew and dreaded the sparkle in Drusilla's eye.

"He is discourteous in persisting when I have made it plain that I dislike his attentions!" Drusilla returned with spirit.

Elizabeth sighed. "His family is one of the most important in Reading, my dear, and James cannot afford to offend them. Although he is a member of the Clothiers' Guild since his uncle died, his business could still be hurt if Jacob Blagrave were to influence his family against us."

"I have no intention of sacrificing myself for the sake of James and his business here!" Drusilla declared angrily. "He is aware that father would prefer him to come home to Devizes and join him in the business now that Edward is dead. Indeed, it was only because James was the second son that father permitted him to come to Reading and join Uncle Robert."

"I know, and James is torn, believe me! He knows that his father depends on him, having no more sons left, and yet he feels that the business here and the transporting of cloth to London, which he is involved in also, will prove more profitable than the woollen business in Devizes."

"Especially if he can persuade me to permit myself to be used as a bribe to Jacob Blagrave!" Drusilla said bitterly, and then bent swiftly to kiss Elizabeth remorsefully, and say that she would take a walk to cool her anger, for she had no wish to quarrel with Elizabeth.

Elizabeth watched her go ruefully. She was finding the charge of her wilful, pretty sister-in-law, only three years younger than herself, too great a burden during the absence of her husband in London. Drusilla had been sent to stay with her brother after she had caused a minor scandal in Devizes by refusing a very advantageous offer from a wealthy merchant in Chippenham and declaring publicly that she had no intention of wedding a man old enough to be her father. That in itself would have been bad enough, for girls were expected to marry where their parents chose, but Drusilla had added to her iniquities by showing an obvious preference for the company of a totally unsuitable young man, Tom Copley, one of her father's own shepherds. In fact, Drusilla had no romantic feelings for this man, but was fascinated by his knowledge of animals and the countryside, and the tales he told her of the people who long ago lived on the downs. However, her determination to seek his company and wander with him over the nearby hills in total disregard of the town's opinion had resulted in this banishment to Reading, and her parents fondly hoped that Elizabeth would succeed in finding a suitable and acceptable husband for their wayward daughter.

It was high time Drusilla was married, Elizabeth mused, for she was by far too attractive for comfort. It was not only her beauty, the dark curling hair and huge, expressive brown eyes set in a softly rounded face, men were drawn to her liveliness and flocked about her. She was never serious for long, but quick to aid anyone in distress, and very determined in pursuit of any objective. At seventeen she needed a husband to control her, but already, after but a few weeks in Reading, she had wilfully rejected the offers of two very worthy men, and now seemed bent on repeating her wayward conduct when, as appeared almost certain, Jacob Blagrave made her an offer.

Already Drusilla's apparent capriciousness, as well as her lively nature and barely concealed contempt for the proprieties, was causing talk in the mainly puritan merchant community, and Elizabeth was well aware that this could adversely affect her reputation, but apart from the occasional remonstrance or warning she forbore to argue with Drusilla, knowing that she would not prevail on her to conduct herself with greater decorum, and praying that James would return before disaster overtook them.

Elizabeth had good reason for her cautious behaviour. Apart from some awe of her sister-in-law, she was again pregnant, and feeling ill and worried. Two earlier pregnancies had ended in miscarriages, and she dreaded a repetition, longing for her husband's comfort on her own account, apart from his authority over Drusilla.

Drusilla had seized a cloak and run out of the house. She found the town in a turmoil, with the citizens anxiously discussing the news of the battle, and she soon realised that Jacob Blagrave's account of it had been unfair to the

11

Royalists. It did not seem, from what details she gleaned, that the Parliamentary army had been so successful as he had maintained. It was unclear which side had been victorious, and since Lord Essex was reported to be in Warwick, while the King was still at the site of the battle, several miles nearer to London, only the optimistic were able to assert with any conviction that Charles had been halted in his march towards the capital.

Indeed, news soon came that Lord Essex had sent anxious letters to Parliament demanding help, and London was preparing fortifications. The King, losing the opportunity for a speedy march to London, went instead to Oxford, and from thence to Reading itself. News of his coming was brought by Meg, who burst unceremoniously into the kitchen one morning where Elizabeth was making pastry for a game pie, and gasped out the news.

"Ma'am, Mistress Drusilla! The Governor, Colonel Marten, has gone! He's fled! They say the King is at the gates! Oh, Ma'am, what shall we do? The King's men will kill us all, or worse!"

Elizabeth, startled, stood speechless while Joan, another maid, who was plucking a fowl, dropped it and put her hands to her mouth to stifle her exclamations of dismay. Drusilla merely laughed in genuine amusement.

"Oh, Meg!" she exclaimed. "Do not be so ridiculous! Since when has King Charles made war on defenceless women?"

"'Tis what they're all saying, Mistress!" Meg declared, offended. "What shall we do? Shall we flee, too, or barricade the house?"

"You may go if you are afeard! For myself, I've a mind to see the King!" Drusilla declared, twirling round and sinking into a deep curtsey.

"Oh, I couldn't leave you to his mercy," Meg said, aghast. "I've heard that the courtiers spare no woman!"

"Pooh! They'll not be interested in us. Elizabeth, I'll go and see what the truth is," she volunteered, untying her apron.

"No, Drusilla!" Elizabeth exclaimed, infected with Meg's fears, but she was soon cajoled into permitting Drusilla, accompanied by one of the grooms, to go forth into the town and discover the

13

truth of the rumours.

It seemed that these were correct, at least in that the King was expected. Walking down to the main branch of the river, Drusilla saw carpenters already at work repairing the drawbridge over the broken arch at Caversham Bridge, and was told by one of the Aldermen that she met there that the King was expected on the following day.

"He plans to treat with Parliament," she was told. "A pity he did not march straight to London when the chance was there."

"Would you have him fight the Londoners?" Drusilla asked in surprise. "I thought the whole Corporation supported the Parliament?"

"Not all of us, by any means. There are plenty who say no good will come of defying the King, for after all, he is King, and we cannot do without him!"

Drusilla was making her way home when she met Mr Blagrave, who greeted her with a doleful face.

"Mistress Drusilla, pray heed my warnings, and do not leave your house while the King is here."

Drusilla tossed her curls. "Why, he is no monster to terrify children," she returned gaily.

Jacob shook his head.

"It is not the King so much as his followers I fear. Not on my own behalf, you understand," he added quickly, "but fear of what they might do to you."

"I think I can take care of myself, Mr Blagrave," Drusilla said coolly.

"Doubtless you do, my dear, but you must permit me to know better, and you must heed my advice. Soldiers are licentious creatures, such as you cannot know, and would have no respect for you."

"You must permit me to act as I deem fit," Drusilla responded, hardly troubling to conceal her anger at his presumption. "You have, after all, no authority over me."

"Not yet," he replied, oblivious of her indignation, "but it is my hope, my very earnest desire, that when your brother returns home I may have the right to guide you."

"You will never have such a right, Mr Blagrave!" Drusilla declared, almost trembling with fury. "Now pray step aside, you block my path!"

He smiled, unperturbed. "Indeed I speak too freely, my dear, and you are right to be angry and chide me. I honour you for your discretion. When is your brother expected back?"

Drusilla surveyed him contemptuously.

"The sooner James returns to depress your expectations the better pleased shall I be," she retorted, and without waiting to see the momentary expression of dismay on his face, pushed past him and almost ran back home.

She was so angry that she told Elizabeth of her encounter as soon as she reached home. Normally she tried to avoid upsetting her sister-in-law, knowing the delicate state of Elizabeth's health, but this time she was too furious to make fun of the affair.

"The impertinence! To give me advice! How dare he presume so!" she raged.

"Indeed he spoke too freely," Elizabeth agreed, "but it would appear nonetheless good advice. We should take care not to venture out of the house if soldiers are to be quartered in the town."

"They are not ogres to frighten babes!" Drusilla laughed, her good humour suddenly restored. "Indeed, life might be vastly more entertaining. I vow I'd rather face a dozen soldiers than Jacob Blagrave!"

Elizabeth shuddered, but forbore to argue the point.

"Why do you dislike the man so?" she asked curiously. "It has reached the state when the mere mention of his name is like to send you into a passion."

Drusilla considered, her head on one side.

"Indeed, I do not fully know," she confessed at last. "The man's a prosy fool, and ancient before he's full grown! He is so pompous, and gives his trite advice so ponderously, as if he were advising the King himself on matters of immense import. Yet it is more than that. I do not trust him. His expression is shifty, he never looks me straight in the eye, but I feel he is always watching to see how I am reacting to what he says, though heaven knows he has been blind enough to my feelings towards him!"

"A mannerism, Dru! He is from a most

estimable family, well respected, wealthy. I — I would not wish you to accept his offer, an he makes one, unless you could respect him, but I am concerned for your reputation. There is too much talk already, and if it is generally known that you have refused so many suitable men, your chances of a good match will be less."

"I cannot help it if men I do not wish to marry make me offers!" Drusilla protested. "No one, however, can accuse me of encouraging them, for I am doing everything in my power, including plain incivility, to deter Mr Blagrave from making any offer! Am I to accept a man simply because he is the third, or fourth, to make an offer? Pray tell me how to prevent unwelcome offers!"

"You will be thought capricious, I fear," Elizabeth said gently. "When suitable men make offers of marriage, you must consider them seriously, for it is no light matter."

"Suitable? Aye, in some sense, but I may not consider them so!"

"What do you want?" Elizabeth asked, puzzled. "You have refused men who are young, handsome, rich, and who would be excellent husbands."

"I want, and indeed intend to marry only a man I can love," Drusilla declared. "Is it my fault that none of the men I have met so far are such?"

"Love is not a sound basis for marriage," Elizabeth said quietly. "Equal fortunes, the same station in life, agreeableness, are all more important than an initial physical attraction, and that, after all, is what the love the poets talk of really consists of. Love comes after marriage, as it did with James and myself. I hardly knew of him before my parents and his uncle arranged the match, and met him only twice before the wedding. Yet now I know that it is an excellent marriage, wisely arranged."

Drusilla considered her pityingly.

"Such would never do for me," she affirmed, "and neither will Jacob Blagrave! I do not trust him, for I think he wishes always to be in the right, and to support those who are powerful and can grant him favours. I have seen him fawning on some of the Aldermen, and the merchants who have the ear of Parliament, for he clearly expects them to triumph over the King. The only time I would willingly see him again is when he realises that the King has finally won, and he changes his tune! Then I'd relish hearing him give his reasons!"

"I wonder if the King will win? What will the end of it be?"

There was no answer to this, but on the following day they had the opportunity of seeing the King ride into Reading with his soldiers, and prepare to take up his residence at Coley House. Immediately the town was plunged into a bustle of activity as tailors from five miles about the town were set to the task of making a thousand suits of uniform. Elizabeth protested vehemently when she was ordered to send the bales of cloth stored in her husband's warehouse for this purpose, but old Tom Farrow, James' chief assistant, advised her to submit and reluctantly she did, on the promise that the cloth would be paid for.

While Elizabeth was dealing with this, Drusilla sat at the parlour window watching the soldiers, hundreds of them, pouring into the town. Then an anguished cry from the left, just outside the window, caused her to open it and lean out. Her eyes widened as she saw Joan, one of the younger maids, struggling to avoid the kisses of one of the soldiers while a couple of his companions laughingly urged him on.

Drusilla looked round her for help, and espied a pair of pistols hung above the court cupboard. They belonged to James, and she had no idea how to use them, or whether they were loaded, but she seized one and ran from the house, pointing it at the man.

"Release her, you villain!" she ordered, and waved the pistol threateningly as he looked at her. Hastily he stepped away from Joan, and the girl, much younger than Drusilla herself, sobbed with relief and hid herself behind Drusilla.

"Go into the house immediately," Drusilla ordered, but Joan cried out in fear.

"They are behind us, too!" she whimpered, and Drusilla saw that the soldier's companions had moved round to stand between her and the door of the house.

21

"Cowards!" she addressed them in a biting tone. "Move out of our way or you'll not live to regret your stupidity!"

They laughed, having recovered from their momentary dismay at seeing such a weapon held in the hands of a girl.

"You'd not hit all of us, my pretty, there'd still be two of us left to deal with you as you deserve," one of them jeered at her, and Drusilla, facing the three of them slowly advancing towards her, a petrified Joan clinging to her skirts, took careful aim at the centre one and pulled the trigger. To her dismay nothing happened, and she stepped back, pushing Joan with her free hand, while the soldiers, now openly laughing, approached more quickly.

Then, to Drusilla's astonishment, they halted, and at the same moment a hand reached down from above her and took the pistol from her grasp.

"If you are to defy the King's command, you ought at least to have your weapons serviceable," an amused voice told her.

She spun round and saw that a cavalry officer had ridden up behind her and was now holding the pistol out of her reach, laughing down at her from a dark, handsome face, his eyes twinkling as he observed her confusion.

"Pray return my property, sir," she demanded, recovering her wits although her heart had begun to pound uncomfortably fast. "When such ruffians as these scum attack defenceless women and children we have need of weapons to protect ourselves!"

"The best defence is to stay indoors, not brandish unloaded pistols," he told her. "Be off to your quarters," he added to the discomfited men, who slunk thankfully away.

"When I need your advice I will be certain to ask for it!" she retorted. "If this is the manner in which the King's troops conduct themselves, then I have much to say for Parliament!"

He laughed, and glanced at her trim figure in the tight fitting blue gown.

"Oh, but they do not appreciate beauty as we do!" he said softly.

"My pistol sir, if you please!" she said, her colour heightened.

"Have you not heard the order?" he asked, dismounting and standing close beside her, so that she suddenly shivered as she looked up at him.

"What order?"

"That all arms are to be taken to the town hall, and if any disobey, their houses are to be sacked."

"Why, that is abominable!" she cried. "We are to be left defenceless while undisciplined rabble such as those men may treat us with discourtesy? Does the King hope to gain adherents in such a manner?"

"No, but he will discover his enemies and render them harmless. The men shall be punished, do not fear, yet it was but a harmless prank, high spirits after the battle!"

"Harmless as yet, if you think frightening Joan harmless! What is to prevent them, or others, from even worse behaviour, when you are not by to deter them, and I have no pistol!"

"Are there no men to protect you?" he asked quickly.

"None but servants. My brother is away."

"I will see to it that you are not molested," he reassured her and looked

24

deep into her eyes, holding her glance so that she could not look away.

"How — how can you do that?" she asked weakly.

"Never mind how, just be certain that none in your house will suffer, and indeed I trust none in the town will either, for there are very few such undisciplined men in our ranks," he added proudly, and Drusilla discovered, to her surprise, that despite the evidence she had of unruly soldiers, she was anxious to believe him.

"Come, if you have any more such pistols, I will take them myself and save any of your maids the necessity of leaving the house. None of you had better stir from it for a day or so. Have you men servants to send when necessary?"

"Yes, of course. The house is here. I heard Joan cry out from inside. There is one more pistol, but that is all. Must we in truth deliver them up?"

"I fear so, but let us hope not for long, as the King will be likely to force terms on the rebels soon. Then you must permit me to teach you how to handle a loaded pistol," he said with a laugh.

"Will you come inside, sir?" she asked shyly.

"Not this time. I beg of you, fetch me the pistol, and I will bring a receipt for them both this evening, if that will serve?"

Drusilla nodded, and swiftly went into the house, returning in a moment with the second pistol. She handed it to the officer and he smiled his thanks, then, with a brief and somehow unsatisfying word of farewell, mounted and rode away, leaving a bemused Drusilla to stand and stare after him until he turned the corner into the High Street and was lost from view.

Reluctantly she turned to re-enter the house, and found Joan watching her with considerable awe.

"Thank you, Mistress Drusilla, for saving me," she whispered, and Drusilla suddenly smiled.

"I was not of great use with an unloaded pistol, was I?" she asked lightly, and sent the girl away to the kitchen, telling her to warn the other maids that they must not leave the house, and then running quietly up the stairs, creeping past Elizabeth's room where her sister-in-law was resting, and on up to her own small room, where she sat down at the window and looked out towards the centre of the town, dreaming idly of laughing eyes deep set in a lean, sun-tanned face, and a warm, caressing voice, and later wondering to herself that she had so meekly permitted a soft-spoken, handsome man to steal not only the pistol she had with her, but persuade her also to hand over the only other weapon which was in the house.

2

DRUSILLA'S musings were abruptly banished as she heard a cry from Elizabeth. For some moments she had been vaguely aware of a confused murmur of voices and opening doors from the first floor of the house, but had unthinkingly assumed that Elizabeth, having finished her rest, was busy there with the maids. Now she heard raised voices, and above the excited tones of Meg and the angry ones of Elizabeth were the deeper tones of a man.

Drusilla flung open the door of her room and ran down the stairs. She discovered Elizabeth standing beside her bed, the coverlet pulled round her shoulders, facing a corporal and two troopers, while a tearful Meg was explaining that she had tried to stop the soldiers but that they had forced their way into the house.

"What do you mean, sirs, by breaking in on my sister so?" Drusilla demanded, running to put her arm about Elizabeth.

"We've no wish to inconvenience the lady, but we've our duty to perform, Mistress, and that's to inspect the houses and billet the right number of troops in each," the corporal said somewhat diffidently.

"Is it necessary to disturb my sister's rest? She is ill!"

"We can't see the house without it, though I'm very sorry to have distressed her," he said apologetically.

"I refuse utterly to have soldiers imposed on me!" Elizabeth declared angrily. "My husband is away, and apart from a couple of servants we have no men to protect us."

"The King's men have to stay somewhere," he explained patiently.

"Not here," was the obdurate reply.

"It must be," he answered, "for we have above three thousand men to accommodate. You cannot refuse, for if you are obstructive I have orders to turn you from the house altogether. Now I propose to inspect the remainder of the house, and I will see you again before I leave to tell you how many men to expect."

So saying, he bowed slightly, gave Drusilla an apologetic glance, and left the room, followed by the reluctant troopers who had been occupied in observing Drusilla appreciatively.

Elizabeth sank down on to the bed and dissolved into weak tears.

"What shall I do?" she moaned. "I cannot bear this!"

Drusilla had been thinking quickly.

"If we are obstinate I believe they will do as they threatened, and turn us out. Do you wish to leave Reading and go to your parents?"

Elizabeth shook her head vehemently.

"No, for it is too far away, I should not be able to protect James' property. I must remain here!"

"Then I fear we must accept them. I have no doubt everyone else will be forced to do so. Three thousand! There are scarcely more of us to begin with! Every house will be made to accommodate two or three men, and larger houses more. A pity that we have those unused rooms! But if we are compliant we shall be treated courteously, and be here to protect the house and ensure that they do not damage aught, or if they do, that they pay for it!" she finished fiercely.

"Mr Blagrave was right, soldiers are despicable!" Elizabeth exclaimed.

"They do what they must," Drusilla said mildly, wondering at her own reasonable attitude, for normally she would have been furiously angry at such an invasion. "Come, let me help you put on your gown, and we will go down to the parlour."

The corporal soon came to them there. He was polite and apologetic, but insisted that half a dozen troopers and their horses must be accommodated.

"We have not so many spare beds!" Elizabeth protested.

"But there is adequate room. I understand that your husband is away on a mission to Parliament." He paused slightly, then continued smoothly. "That being so, he is scarce likely to return while the King remains in Reading. You can move into your sister's room with her, and we will put a couple of pallet beds in your room, which is large."

"No!" Drusilla exclaimed angrily while Elizabeth, too aghast to speak, leaned back in the chair where she sat, putting her hands to her face in despair.

"It is the only way to get the required number of beds, Mistress," the harassed man was explaining, scratching his head, but Drusilla did not permit him to finish.

"If you must billet your men on us they will have to make do with what rooms are empty! You have no right to force my sister out of her own bed!"

One of the troopers standing by the door sniggered.

"I'd be willing to share it with her," he offered, while his companion, moving a step into the room, leered at Drusilla.

"I'll settle for the other, even if her bed is smaller," he chuckled. "It'd be more friendly!"

Drusilla, her fists clenched, turned towards him but was prevented from replying as Elizabeth gave a faint moan and fell sideways, and would have slipped to the floor had not the corporal suddenly flung himself forward to support her. Drusilla turned quickly, realised that Elizabeth had fainted, and bent down towards her.

"Get those — scum — out of here!"

32

she ordered through clenched teeth at the corporal, and the troopers, somewhat dismayed at the results of their attempted gallantry, hastened to efface themselves. Drusilla chaffed Elizabeth's hands and called for Meg who, having been hovering anxiously outside the door, came immediately.

"Help me carry your mistress upstairs," Drusilla ordered, but the corporal, a large man, shook his head.

"Lasses like you cannot manage. Will you permit me?"

Drusilla nodded and led the way, thanking the corporal curtly when he had laid Elizabeth down on the bed.

"If she sees those two ruffians again, I'll not answer for the consequences!" she told him.

"I offer my sincere apologies, Mistress. I will see to it that you have decent men!"

"It will be well for you that you do!"

He somehow got himself out of the room, and Meg and Drusilla soon had Elizabeth, recovered from her swoon, tucked up in bed. Meg, fetching a posset for Elizabeth, reported that a different

33

trooper, a pleasant, well-mannered man, was stationed in the kitchen, and had advised her that no one should leave the house until the town was better organised.

"He offered to escort us if we had need to go out," she added with a simper, and was plainly reconciled to his presence.

Elizabeth, however, was still distressed, and nothing Drusilla could say consoled her. She insisted that she would not have strange men, wicked soldiers, in the house, and grew hysterical when Drusilla attempted to convince her that they had no alternative. Eventually Drusilla, desperate, suggested that they should appeal directly to the King, and Elizabeth, too much beside herself with anxiety to think clearly, begged her to go to him at once.

As yet there was but the one trooper in the house, and Drusilla, wanting no escort, set the willing Meg to the task of distracting him while she slipped out of the house and took her mare from the stables. Once out in the street she made her way as quickly as the milling crowds of citizens and soldiers would permit to Coley House, on the hills to the south of the town. At last she came to the house and found the courtyard crowded with soldiers and civilians, some rushing importantly about, others idling, and many patiently waiting for audience with the King, either from curiosity, or because they had petitions to present.

In all the confusion there was no one to be found with whom she could leave the mare, and so Drusilla dismounted and tied the reins to a ring in the wall, then, realising in some dismay the magnitude of the task she had set herself, she wove her way through the multitude towards the main door of the house, guarded by two soldiers.

Drusilla approached hesitantly, but they were busy examining the credentials of a couple of men who were gesticulating wildly and demanding to be admitted, and she had to wait. Several officers passed through the door, with nods of recognition from the guards, and some of the members of the Town Corporation, escorted by two officers, were taken in, much to the displeasure of the angry couple still arguing with the guards, who demanded why they should be made to wait.

"His Majesty has important business," one of the guards repeated wearily, and turned to Drusilla, but just at that moment the officer who had earlier rescued her from the troopers and then taken her pistol appeared in the doorway, and she halted, looking at him as if she could not believe her eyes. He lifted his eyebrows slightly, then inclined his head in recognition and came towards her, smiling in what she found to be a most disturbing manner.

"Did you not trust me to bring the receipts?" he asked with a laugh, and for a moment Drusilla stared at him uncomprehendingly. Then she smiled back at him and shook her head quickly.

"I came on quite another matter. Indeed, how should I have known to find you here?"

"I trust it is no great disappointment! In what may I be of service?" he asked, taking her unresisting arm and drawing her away from the doorway and into a corner where they could speak privately.

"I came to see the King," Drusilla replied, with what she afterwards chided herself was idiotic simplicity.

"To be sure, as have half the town, it would seem. But was it mere idle curiosity?"

"Of course not!" she said shortly, recovering her poise. "My sister-in-law, who is ill, has been subjected to the most inconsiderate invasion of her house, threatened and intolerably abused!"

"How is this?" he demanded, and Drusilla, stealing a glance at his suddenly narrowed eyes and frowning countenance, shivered, and thought how unnerving it would be were she to find herself the subject of his displeasure.

She told him of the way in which the demands for beds for the soldiers had been made, of how the corporal, though polite, had forced his way into Elizabeth's room, and then suggested turning her out of it. Blushing, she recounted the coarse suggestions of the troopers and the unfortunate result on Elizabeth.

"I fear that she will miscarry again, she is so distressed, and I came to beg the King not to force these men, or indeed any of these despicable soldiers, into her house. The corporal promised that he would send decent men, but how can I trust in his promises, for they all seem ruffianly! Besides, Elizabeth grows hysterical at the very idea, and I cannot persuade her that we have no choice!"

He regarded her thoughtfully for a moment.

"You have no men in the house, I collect, apart from servants. Do they sleep in the house?"

"No, in the stable loft."

"It is impossible to make your sister-in-law an exception, for many others would also demand preferential treatment, but I have a suggestion. Would she be willing to accommodate women?"

"Camp followers!" Drusilla exclaimed in horror. "That would be even more of an insult!"

"Not all camp followers are disreputable," he said, laughing down at her. "I am thinking of a lady newly arrived here, having been on her way from London to join her husband whom she thought to find in Oxford. Their house is too close to London for safety, and she has left it together with her three young children and her maid. Would your sister take pity on them, and the husband and his manservant? I do not think Captain Rogers and his family would be a threat or an insult to her!"

"That would indeed be a solution, and I am sure I can bring her to agree," Drusilla exclaimed gratefully, her eyes shining. "Oh, that is most kind, sir!"

"Then if you will await me here for a few minutes while I make the necessary arrangements, I will escort you home and explain the matter personally to your sister-in-law. Will you take a glass of wine with me first?"

"Thank you, but I prefer to return as quickly as possible, for Elizabeth will be uneasy until I do."

He nodded, and went swiftly back into the house. Within the space of a remarkably short time he reappeared, helped Drusilla mount her horse, and was riding beside her back into the town.

Drusilla took careful stock of him as they went, and he chatted lightly about what they saw. In his late twenties, he was tall with broad shoulders and a slim but muscular body. Clothed in expensive, well-cut coat and breeches, he sat his horse as though he had been born in the saddle and Drusilla, no mean horsewoman, recognised the skill with which he effortlessly controlled his highly bred, spirited mount. His face was lean and tanned, with widely spaced laughing blue eyes, prominent cheekbones and an aquiline nose. His mobile mouth showed white, even teeth when he smiled, which seemed to be often. Dark curled hair was surmounted by a broad brimmed hat which sported a gaily waving plume. That and a jaunty moustache added the final touch to a dashing, attractive picture.

"Are you aware that we have not as yet introduced ourselves?" he asked suddenly, breaking into her reflections. "I cannot but feel that your sister would accept me more readily if you were able to present me with due formality!"

Drusilla laughed and agreed.

"I am Drusilla Matthews," she informed him. "I live in Devizes, where my father is a woollen merchant, but I am staying with my brother James, who at the moment is — " she paused, suddenly aware that it might not be politic to tell a Royalist of her brother's activities, then went on quickly, " — is away from home."

He appeared not to have noticed her hesitation.

"Sir Randal Thornton, of Thornton Hall, near Abingdon, at your service," he replied. "Is your brother a woollen merchant, too?"

"A clothier. He was the second son, and when my uncle, who was childless, offered to make him his heir, my father agreed. Then Edward, my elder brother, died of smallpox last year and so James will have both businesses."

Chatting easily they rode on side by side until they were only a hundred yards from the house, when the shocked voice of Mr Blagrave smote Drusilla's ears.

"Mistress Drusilla!" he exclaimed, stepping into the roadway and seizing the bridle so that she was forced to stop. "What in the world has happened?" he demanded, glaring at Sir Randal, who looked him up and down in some amusement.

"How dare you!" Drusilla exclaimed. "Release my horse immediately!"

41

"I will escort you home, Mistress, for it is hardly wise for you to be alone in the streets with the situation as it is!"

"You will do nought of the kind! I have adequate protection, I thank you, and do not require yours!"

"Nevertheless I could not reconcile it with my conscience to permit you to ride without my escort. What will your brother say when he returns?"

Drusilla gritted her teeth.

"Since you know nought of the circumstances, I trust he will tell you not to interfere in what does not concern you!" she snapped.

"But what you do is very much my concern," he replied, impervious to her snub. "I promised James that I would see to it that you came to no harm while he was in London, and I intend to keep that promise."

Drusilla was about to reply angrily when she realised that Sir Randal had quietly turned his horse and was coming forward so that the horse's nose almost touched that of the mare, who stretched her neck out inquisitively towards him.

Fascinated she watched as, when Jacob Blagrave was pulled momentarily from his balance, Sir Randal quickly manoeuvred his horse's head between the mare and him, so that he was forced to release the bridle or be trampled on. The intelligent steed even attempted to nip the hand that held the bridle, but it was snatched away in time, and suddenly Sir Randal was blocking her view of Mr Blagrave as he turned in a circle so that they could continue on their way. Stifling her laughter she cast a glance brimful of merriment at Sir Randal, and lost no time in urging the mare to a trot.

"That was masterly," she gasped when they were out of earshot of Mr Blagrave's indignant protests. "He will be absolutely rigid with anger!"

"Who was your overweening friend?"

"A pompous, tedious ass!" she replied. "Jacob Blagrave, whose family is very important here. He is only a very distant cousin, but he behaves as though the whole town exists at his bidding and for his pleasure. I am horribly afraid he intends to make me an offer, for his hints are too obvious to be ignored, and I shall be in disgrace with James when I refuse someone else."

"You make a habit of refusing offers?" he queried, laughing, and Drusilla blushed.

"Well, no one I liked, only old, and worthy men have made me offers!" she retorted.

"Are the young — and unworthy — men of Devizes and Reading so blind?"

Drusilla gurgled, blushed again, and thankfully announced that they had arrived. She led the way along a narrow lane to the stable entrance, and gave the horses into the charge of Willy, the elderly groom, who whistled through an almost toothless jaw in admiration of Sir Randal's horse. Leaving him rapt in bliss at the prospect of dealing with such a magnificent animal, Drusilla took Sir Randal unceremoniously through the kitchen, and there discovered from Meg, whose eyes grew as round at the sight of Sir Randal as Willy's had at the sight of his horse, that Elizabeth was calmer now and had insisted on dressing.

"She is sitting in the parlour, Mistress,

thinking to protect the house from the soldiers, poor dear, while you are gone."

"Shall I go to her first and explain?" Drusilla asked, turning to Sir Randal, but he shook his head and smiled reassuringly.

"I promise I will not upset her. Take me in and introduce me, and leave the explanations to me," he said calmly, and Drusilla nodded and went on ahead.

At first, Elizabeth was inclined to resent Sir Randal's visit, regarding it as yet another imposition, but he sympathised so readily with her grievances, apologising on behalf of his fellow soldiers, and promising that they should not go unpunished for their impertinence, that she began to treat him with positive friendliness, and when he told her of the unfortunate plight of Captain Rogers and his family, she needed little persuasion to reach the conclusion that to house that family would be far more satisfactory to her than to fight unavailingly to keep her house to herself. Drusilla was left with the strong suspicion that Elizabeth considered that she had herself made the suggestion, and was highly amused as she watched her sister succumbing to the practised charm of Sir Randal. Then he caught her eye upon him and winked, most reprehensively, at her, causing her to colour up in confusion and hurriedly drop her gaze.

"The King proposes to march towards London within a few days, Mistress Matthews," Sir Randal explained. "He expects to treat there with Parliament, and the major part of the soldiers will go with him. I expect that as soon as Captain Rogers can arrange for lodgings in Oxford, he will remove his family there and you will be left in peace."

Elizabeth smiled wanly, but assured him that she would be only too happy to give what help she could to the Rogers family, and within an hour Sir Randal had brought them to her: Mistress Rogers tearfully grateful to Elizabeth, and the children, aged from two to six years, still quiet and bewildered at the sudden disturbance in their previously orderly existences.

While Elizabeth occupied herself in comforting the children, and seeing them fed, Drusilla took Mistress Rogers to the rooms Elizabeth had set aside for them, and helped her to unpack the few possessions she had managed to bring away with her. She was a small, lively woman, and gave Drusilla an account of the difficulties she had experienced, first from the attitude of her neighbours, who had all supported Parliament, and had been most offensive when they had discovered that her husband had joined the King, and then from the journey, with only her maid and a single groom to aid her. She spoke of the enormous relief she had felt when she had heard that the King's army was at Reading, and on turning aside had been fortunate to meet her husband almost at once. She knew of the King's plan to march towards London, and was most anxious that her husband might be permitted to stay and escort her to Oxford.

"For I cannot wish to impose on dear Mistress Matthews for longer than is absolutely essential," she asserted.

When she repeated this to Elizabeth after the exhausted children had been put to bed, Elizabeth quickly reassured her, and had so recovered her spirits as to be able to laugh when she told Mistress

Rogers of the unwelcome alternative she had been spared. Captain Rogers soon appeared, embarrassingly grateful to Elizabeth, and they all sat down to supper, which proved to be a merry meal.

On the following morning Elizabeth and Mistress Rogers were talking in the parlour while Drusilla, sitting with some sewing in her hands, was lost in a world of dreams from which she emerged with occasional starts to set another few stitches, before her hands again grew idle and she sat, a smile trembling on her lips, recalling every word that she and Sir Randal had exchanged, and every look on his handsome face.

These pleasant thoughts were shattered when Meg came in to announce that Mr Blagrave had called, and Drusilla moved quickly to sit in a solitary chair beside the window before he could enter the room.

For some time he chatted inconsequentially, and then informed the ladies that the King proposed moving from the town shortly. Since he was unaware of Mistress Rogers' connection with the army, and had assumed her to be a visiting friend, he was visibly put out when he found that the ladies knew more of these proposals than he did himself. Before the cause could be explained to him, Meg, considerably flustered, announced another caller.

"Sir Randal Thornton, Mistress!" she said in some awe, and he followed her into the room to be greeted with enthusiasm by all the ladies, and cold, somewhat astonished civility by Mr Blagrave.

Drusilla watched them curiously, wondering how they would refer to the encounter of the previous day, but when Sir Randal laughingly apologised for his horse's apparent bad manners it was clear that Mr Blagrave preferred to ignore the incident, since he looked blankly at Sir Randal, then pursed his lips before turning back towards Elizabeth.

Sir Randal, regarding him with a derisive eye, chatted for a few minutes with Mistress Rogers and then, seeing that there was no seat near Drusilla, calmly picked up a chair and came to sit beside her, to the obvious annoyance of Mr Blagrave.

"I came to ask you to walk out with me, to show me the town, Mistress Drusilla,"

Sir Randal said softly after a while.

"I — I should be honoured," Drusilla replied, somewhat breathlessly.

"Then let us ask your sister-in-law's permission at once, and escape while the good Mr Blagrave holds her attention," he suggested audaciously, and suited his actions to his words, scarcely giving Elizabeth time to consider his suggestion before he had whisked Drusilla out of the room, leaving Jacob Blagrave, disapproving but impotent, to listen scowlingly to the effusions of the two ladies, who had nought but admiration to lavish on Sir Randal.

"He seems very taken with your dear Drusilla," Mistress Rogers commented. "It would be quite a triumph for her to attach him, for he is a wealthy man, and high in the councils of the Prince Rupert."

"A courtier?" Mr Blagrave asked, his tone leaving no doubt of his opinion of courtiers.

"Yes, sir, and very much sought after by the ladies. He is exceedingly popular."

"H'm. A trifler, no doubt, merely amusing himself at the expense of a young, inexperienced girl. If you take my advice, Mistress Matthews, you'll warn Mistress Drusilla to be wary of him."

"Drusilla knows her own mind, Mr Blagrave," Elizabeth said sharply, for even she was growing tired of the young man's presumption.

"Sir Randal is no trifler, but is undoubtedly attractive. He has for ten years resisted all the lures thrown out to him. That is why I said it would be a triumph were Mistress Drusilla to capture him, but she is lovely enough, and good-natured enough to succeed, and indeed I hope she may," Mistress Rogers commented, and turned to regale Elizabeth with stories of the Court, which she knew from before her own marriage, leaving Mr Blagrave a prey to the direst anxiety.

If he could have seen the excellent terms Drusilla and Sir Randal were on, he would have had even more cause to lose hope. Sir Randal, with his address and charm, soon banished the last lingering shyness Drusilla felt for him. They wandered in the meadows beside the river, talking together about many topics, though afterwards Drusilla could recall little of what they said, only the delight she had found in his company. It was with considerable surprise that she realised how far they had come when he eventually suggested turning back.

"Indeed we must return, or I shall be late for dinner," she said reluctantly, and looked longingly towards the distant hills, wishing that they could walk all day without interruption.

They were almost home when Drusilla's dreams collapsed at Sir Randal's news that he was leaving on the following day. She turned a dismayed face to him, and he smiled wryly.

"What will happen now?" she asked. "Does the King leave, too?"

"He is hoping to meet a deputation from Parliament. If matters can be agreed, no doubt we will move into London. If not — " he shrugged. "Who knows? They might decide to fight there, or the King may prefer to withdraw for the winter to some strongly fortified town. If no agreement is reached, I cannot see a speedy end to the war."

"Reading is not strongly fortified,"

Drusilla said slowly. "Are we in danger of attack by Parliament?"

"None can tell. But as it guards the river and the gap in the hills, the King will wish to make it secure. If the treating fails, you will see us back in Reading soon, I have little doubt."

They had reached the door, and though Drusilla, wistful and confused, invited him in, he refused, saying that he had much to do and begging her to make his apologies to Mistress Matthews. With a gay smile and a wave of the hand he was gone, and Drusilla stood looking after him, bemused, until the realisation that she was cold caused her to turn and enter the house.

She was bewildered and disturbed by the tumultuous feelings aroused in her by his entrance into her life. He was handsome, young and charming, a man of resource and easy command, yet a delightful companion. She knew that she had never met his like before, and he had made so profound an impression on her that she had thought of little apart from him since the first encounter. Was this love? She was unsure, and the manner of his departure, with no definite promise of ever seeing her again, made her wary of misreading the admiration she had seen in his eyes when he looked at her. She had no need of the warnings Elizabeth, worried by her abstraction, proffered about the placing of too much reliance on attractive men, courted as they must be by many rich and lovely women. Only too well did she realise the impossibility of a rich, handsome, titled young man considering marriage with the daughter of a merchant, even though a prosperous and ambitious one, but the mere glimpse of what life could have been with a man such as Sir Randal made her even more determined to resist the offers of Jacob Blagrave and his kind.

3

SIR RANDAL did not come again, although Drusilla hoped that he would appear on the following morning. Instead she had to suffer the peevish complaints of the jealous Mr Blagrave, who seemed genuinely puzzled to find that a girl could apparently prefer the attentions of a fine feathered courtier to the company of a solid, worthy man such as he knew himself to be.

"It was not wise, my dear Drusilla, to walk alone with such a man, for your reputation will suffer," he chided.

"I am not your dear Drusilla," the lady informed him sharply. "As for my reputation, that is my affair, I think!"

He laughed, uncertain of whether to contradict her.

"Well, as to that, we will see when your brother returns. I imagine it is youthful high spirits which makes you behave with so little discretion. We have all discovered the temptations of youth," he admitted, sublimely unconscious that he himself, for ever old in spirit, had not been in the slightest troubled by any desire to behave other than comfortably.

At last his strictures drove Drusilla out of the room, with a muttered excuse that she felt unwell. Elizabeth, beginning to appreciate her objections to Mr Blagrave now that he became bolder in his assumptions of eventual success with Drusilla, and, although she did not realise this, after experiencing the charm of Sir Randal, tried to give Mr Blagrave a gentle warning.

"Drusilla has a lively nature," she said carefully. "It is no fault other than heedlessness, but she will never, I think, be driven."

"She needs firm guidance," he replied kindly.

"Her parents will never force her into an unwelcome match," Elizabeth said more sharply.

He was oblivious.

"Girls of her age are not the best judges of what is wise for them. When is your husband expected back, Mistress Matthews? I would wish to speak with him as soon as is convenient."

"I have not heard," Elizabeth replied, with a sigh both for his obtuseness and her own loneliness.

At length he took himself off, and since Drusilla was in a decidedly prickly mood, Elizabeth forbore to probe into whether any indication had been given by Sir Randal that he intended to pay more visits.

The King and most of his troops moved out of Reading, and news trickled back of events nearer the capital. Since Windsor Castle had been occupied by Parliament, and an attack by Prince Rupert failed, the King went via Egham to Colnbrook, there to discuss with the Parliamentary Commissioners arrangements for a conference. Lord Essex, back in London after Edge Hill battle, marched out towards the King with the London Trained Bands, while the King moved to Brentford. The events there were described by Captain Rogers, who returned to Reading a few days later.

"With Parliament on the march, what were we to think but that they considered the truce at an end? The Prince attacked early in the morning and soon overcame the defenders, but the success unfortunately went to the heads of the younger and wilder men, and they were not to be controlled. Some unnecessary damage was done," he admitted, but it was only later that they heard from an indignant Mr Blagrave of the houses fired, the wine and linen and plate looted, thatch burned and windows broken, as well as a few assaults on citizens.

"They are animals!" Drusilla declared, and Elizabeth shuddered, praying that they would all keep away from Reading.

Captain Rogers described how the King had advanced to Turnham Green, but finding Essex too deeply entrenched in a favourable position, and well supplied from London, while his own troops were weary and feeling the effects of long marches in the November cold, withdrew.

"He returns to Reading," Captain Rogers informed them. "I am to go on to Oxford, and there hope to find suitable lodgings so that you will be relieved of my family, Mistress Matthews, in a very short while."

The brief respite from occupation by

the troops was over. Drusilla, angered by the reports she had heard of the behaviour of the Royalists at Brentford, was torn between her fears of renewed impositions, especially when Elizabeth no longer had the excuse of housing the Rogers family, and her longing to see Sir Randal again. During his brief absence she had accepted that she had fallen in love with him, and could never forget him. She suspected that on his part it had been nought but a pleasant flirtatious interlude, and dejectedly told herself that she was being foolish to dream that anything more could come of it. Even if, unlikely as it seemed, he did love her, such a man as Sir Randal, rich, well born, powerful and much sought after by women of his own class, would never consider allying himself with the daughter of a woollen merchant.

On the following day, Elizabeth was overjoyed when James appeared, and poured out to him all the troubles and fears she had borne during his absence. His anger so frightened her that she then turned to pleading with him not to rash be when he threatened vengeance on those responsible for distressing her.

"My dear, it is over now, and you are here again, which is all that matters," she urged.

"But it not over," he pointed out. "Already we are being expected to pay seven pounds each week to support Sir Arthur Aston, the new Governor, and the King is to return, which will cost us a deal more I have no doubt. Where will our businesses be when we are taxed of all our profits?"

However, he seemed content to remain at home, watching developments, and Elizabeth's fears gradually subsided. The King returned, and when an order for the town to raise two hundred pounds a week for the King's expenses and to supply the greatly enlarged garrison was announced, James fumed quietly at home, but to Elizabeth's relief seemed unwilling to protest publicly.

Drusilla was less easily satisfied than Elizabeth, who thought that James had overcome his resentment, and solved the riddle of her brother's uncharacteristically meek behaviour when she spoke with a neighbour who was complaining bitterly

60

of the necessity of working on the fortifications which were being thrown up around the town.

"It is monstrous!" Mr Tanner declared. "All must work on pain of a fine of sevenpence a day. Who can afford that? A day's work for eightpence, that is all they pay, and we lose our workmen while the money for the wages comes from taxing us! And should we dare to complain we are assessed for more fines and forced loans! Your brother had best have a care. He is already a marked man, having been with the deputation, and stands to lose all his possessions if he speaks a word against the King!"

Drusilla watched with mounting anger as more demands were made, buildings requisitioned, and soldiers installed in the Oracle, formerly a charity for poor clothiers. She even consented to accompany Mr Blagrave on a walk about the town, so anxious was she to see precisely what was happening.

"The River Kennet and the marshy ground are some protection to the south," Jacob explained, encouraged to think that Drusilla, with her growing anger against the King, was becoming more amenable to his attentions. "We will go first to see what is being done at Harrison's Barn, to the southeast."

"That is well outside the town," Drusilla commented.

"And guards the road from London. Do you see the redoubt at the junction of the three roads?" he asked, pointing it out to her, and she nodded.

"Have the roads been damaged deliberately?" she asked, indicating the gaping holes which were far larger than the ruts and holes which normally made travel by road uncomfortable.

"To hinder the advance, as is the purpose of those iron engines scattered in the fields to stop the horses," he said.

They moved on to the north, where the River Thames bounded the town, and already there were deep ditches dug and earthworks thrown up.

"They propose to blow up the nave of the Abbey to obtain stone for the defences," Jacob said as they crossed the Abbey Bridge over the River Kennet and came in sight of this partially ruined church.

"Will they destroy the whole town?" Drusilla demanded.

"Aye, if we cannot prevent it by a speedy victory," Jacob said gloomily.

Drusilla's anger was increased as she saw the carpenters who were working to make the centre of Caversham Bridge into a drawbridge halt while two strings of pack ponies carrying bundles of firewood were led across.

"For the garrison, supplied free," she was told.

Further round, to the west side of the town, posts and chains had been erected across the ends of the streets. Drusilla turned away, sick at the realisation of how war interfered with the normal lives of people only indirectly involved, and paid little heed to the continuing fulminations of Mr Blagrave. Her musings were interrupted as they were returning to the centre of the town by whoops of glee coming from a large group of boys running towards them.

"What are they doing out of school?" Jacob frowned, and grasped one of the smaller boys to demand of him the answer to his question.

"School's been rec — rec — taken over to be used to keep powder in, sir," the lad gasped, "so we've no more lessons! To horse! To horse!" he yelled, and tore himself free of Jacob's grasp to hurtle after his companions.

At the look of dismay on Jacob's face Drusilla's mood suddenly changed.

"It is not then all bad," she said with a laugh. "They at least are happy at the turn of events!"

"But the disruption to their schooling — the indiscipline that will be engendered," Jacob protested, destroying the better understanding that seemed to have been growing between them, for he would not admit that a holiday could do little harm.

When Drusilla returned home, she found Mistress Rogers in a flutter of anticipation, having received word that her husband would be taking her to Oxford on the following day.

"The King will return there soon, no doubt," she said in great excitement, "and the Court will be gay this winter. Such a pity if the poor Prince Charles is too unwell to travel."

"Is he ill?" Elizabeth asked, quick with sympathy for any child.

"Measles," Mistress Rogers told her. "I live in fear that my own darlings will catch it if there is an epidemic in the town, and so, much as I regret leaving you after all your kindnesses, I cannot help being relieved that we are to go so soon."

When they had departed the house seemed empty, and James became more and more worried as he watched the growing ascendancy of the Royalist faction on the Corporation.

"They are agreeing to all the pernicious demands that are made!" he complained at supper one night. "The Mayor and his lackeys have crawled to Coley House and meekly agreed to pay all that is asked, regardless of what we can afford!"

"The King will be gone soon," Elizabeth tried to console him.

"Aye, but the demands will remain!" he predicted, and indeed it seemed to make no difference when the King and his retinue left at the end of November.

It was to distract him from gloomy forebodings one evening that Elizabeth showed him a letter she had just received from Mistress Rogers, now installed in Oxford. After complaining of the cramped lodgings that were all that were to be found in the crowded city, she went on to describe the busy social life. James was glancing cursorily over the letter when his attention was suddenly caught.

"What's this about Drusilla?" he demanded, and looked across at his sister suspiciously. "Who is this Sir Randal Thornton?"

"What does it say?" Drusilla demanded, for she had not read the letter.

James referred to it.

"'I met Sir Randal Thornton again last night, and he asked how you were. It appears that he is making up to a cousin of Lord Percy, so we were wrong in thinking that he might have been interested in Drusilla. A pity, for I really think he might have settled on the dear girl if he had been given the opportunity of knowing her for longer.'

"Well, sister?"

"Well, brother?" she replied composedly, although her heart was thumping painfully against her ribs. "Am I to be held responsible for the speculations of every gossip?"

"There is always some foundation for gossip. Who is this man, and what has he to do with you?"

"He was an officer who helped us," Elizabeth interposed hurriedly. "He learned of the insults we had been offered, and made the arrangements for Mistress Rogers to be placed with us. I did tell you when you came home."

"But why this vulgar reference to his interest in Drusilla?"

"He was merely a charming, friendly man," Elizabeth explained, "and Mistress Rogers has read too much into normal politeness."

James had to be satisfied, but he made several scathing remarks about Drusilla's predilection for unsuitable men, and opined that the sooner she was wed the better for everyone. Drusilla bore it all calmly, trying not to show the hurt the news had caused her. No matter how often she told herself that it was ridiculous to imagine that the attentions of Sir Randal had been anything more than the normal manner of a courtier, she was wounded by this proof that she was correct.

She was still unwilling, however, to listen to the offer of Jacob Blagrave. When he met her while she was out shopping one morning, and escorted her home, she was curt to the point of rudeness.

"I have business with your brother," he said, falling into step beside her. "I imagine that you can guess what that might be?"

"I cannot surmise," she replied coldly, "unless it is to discuss with him ways of avoiding the fines levied. I see that you are not working on the fortifications?"

"Can you envisage me doing that?" he scoffed. "No, my dear, I pay my sevenpence a day and consider myself fortunate. After all, I suppose the war has to be paid for, and a settlement will be of benefit to the country, so we must all make some sacrifices."

"Do you become a Royalist?" she asked in some amazement.

He laughed self-consciously.

"Not so, my dear, but business will

suffer if we are too obdurate."

"James will hardly agree with you!"

"Since that is not to be the subject of our talk, I cannot say. I hope I may see you later, Mistress Drusilla, when I have settled matters satisfactorily with your brother?"

"I can see no purpose in it," Drusilla returned, and went to find Elizabeth and complain about his impertinence. She begged Elizabeth to persuade James to inform Mr Blagrave that she would never be willing to accept any offer from him, and reluctantly Elizabeth promised to make the attempt, while pointing out that she was unlikely to succeed since James firmly believed that women should have no say in such matters.

It was therefore with no surprise that she found James telling her on the following day that he had accepted Mr Blagrave's offer for her hand.

"A most estimable young man, with a satisfactory fortune, and even better prospects," he said complacently. "This will be a most useful alliance for me, my dear sister, and you can consider yourself fortunate to have won such a man. It is exactly what father wished when you came to Reading."

"Oh, no, James," Drusilla responded. "I have no intention of wedding Jacob Blagrave, and so I shall tell him if he has the impudence to speak to me. Besides, it is not for you to give permission, that is for father."

"Normally, yes, but father had shown sufficient trust in me to depute that task to me. After the scandal you made in Devizes no one there would consider taking you, and it is fortunate, after your capricious actions here in refusing two good offers, that Mr Blagrave is willing to overlook your behaviour and still take you. Your chances will diminish if you reject him, and with the war now likely to continue for some time longer it is urgent to see you settled."

"Are my wishes to be totally ignored?"

"You cannot know what is good for you. Are you dreaming of some highborn lord? Do not be foolish, sister, they do not marry with merchant stock. Even father, who has been so ambitious for you, did not aspire to wed you so far above us. I can see that this Sir Randal Thornton has much to answer for if he had filled your head with romantic nonsense!"

"I am aware of my limitations, James, and do not wish for the moon!" Drusilla retorted. "I merely ask to marry a man I can respect, not a pompous bore who drives me to distraction within a few minutes of enduring his company!"

"You are still a child!" James exclaimed, and seeing that she would not change his views, Drusilla flung out of the room, knowing that though her dream of Sir Randal was hopeless, she would still refuse to marry Jacob Blagrave.

Mr Blagrave did not entertain any such doubts, for on the same day he appeared to inform Drusilla that it was all settled, and that he had written to her parents. As if conferring an honour he announced that they would soon be wed.

"You mistake, for I will never marry you," Drusilla stated flatly, but he listened to her no more than had James.

"A natural reluctance on the part of a maid to consider such matters," he said complacently. "There must be some delay, I fear, for James wishes us to be married here in Reading, and yet the state of

Elizabeth's health prevents it for a few months. Your parents will wish to travel here, too, and that will not be possible until the worst of the winter is over. A June wedding would be charming, do you not agree?"

"Never, in June or any other time!" Drusilla repeated, and when she threatened to run away rather than be constrained into such an unwelcome match, he merely laughed at her for the child he chose to consider her.

Before Drusilla could make any further attempt to convince James that she was in earnest, his own affairs took a turn for the worse. Already noted as a member of the deputation, he had been trying to live as quietly as possible, but then he was informed that as a 'Roundhead rebel' he was to be taxed thrice the amount of others. To avoid this he declared that he must leave Reading, and one dark night he slipped away, intending to join the Parliamentary army.

Drusilla was sorry to see him go, for she had considerable affection for him despite his obduracy regarding her own affairs, and knew besides that Elizabeth would suffer intensely, but at least it halted the progress of her own projected marriage and for that she could not be other than thankful. She had written an impassioned plea to her parents begging them to refuse the hateful match, but they had replied that she was to obey James and do as he thought fit.

'We took heed of your views before, my dear,' her mother wrote, 'but there can be no real objection to this young man and the marriage must be. I hope to find you in better spirits when we come to Reading in the spring.'

She went on to speak mainly of Elizabeth's hopes of bearing this child, telling Drusilla that she must do nought to distress her sister-in-law, and must try to help her and make Elizabeth rest as much as possible.

Sighing, Drusilla resorted to making what excuses she could to avoid Mr Blagrave's company, losing no opportunity of informing him that she was not willing to agree to her brother's plans, but he seemed as impervious to direct statements as he had earlier been to hints, and she could only hope that some change in the war might save her.

In December there was some excitement in the town when it was learned that Prince Rupert, whose prowess as a cavalry leader was already well known and who was famous for his exploits abroad, as well as being, at only twenty-three, the most experienced of the Royalist commanders, was coming to Reading. Even Elizabeth, missing James severely, took an interest in the preparations that were being made by the Mayor to entertain the Prince to a banquet.

"He is borrowing plate from all who are willing to lend it," she reported. "Mr Blagrave told me this morning, while you were out, my dear, of all the pieces his family are lending."

"So they are courting favour with the Royalists now, are they?" Drusilla asked scornfully. "But a few weeks back Jacob Blagrave had nought good to say of any of them, yet now he is buying favours!"

"The Mayor wishes to make a good display," Elizabeth pleaded, but Drusilla merely scoffed at their pretension.

On the day after the banquet Drusilla went out, wrapping herself against the bitter cold in a blue velvet cloak, and walked near the Abbey. She was watching, as had become her custom, the progress of the work on the fortifications when a familiar voice that she had thought never to hear again spoke close to her ear. Swinging round in amazement she found Sir Randal, dressed in vastly elegant clothes, and with a dashing, curly brimmed hat on his head, smiling down at her.

"I hoped that I might have the pleasure of seeing you, Mistress Drusilla," he said, and Drusilla's heart leaped joyfully at the sound until she sternly reminded herself of the cousin of Lord Percy, to whom Sir Randal was paying such marked attentions in Oxford.

"I had not heard that you were in Reading, Sir Randal," she said as coolly as she was able. "Did you accompany the Prince?"

"I came to join him here, and arrived just in time for the Mayor's banquet last night," he replied, frowning slightly at her coldness.

"I trust that you had an enjoyable time," Drusilla commented. "The fortification of Reading goes on apace, you see. Do you imagine that all the money we have been forced to spend will keep out the wicked Parliamentarian soldiers?"

"You speak as though you would be glad to see them here," he said calmly.

She shook her head.

"We desire no armies here," she said bleakly. "Did the Mayor give you the impression that you were welcome?"

"He made a fair attempt," Sir Randal replied, "until he realised that he had made a mistake in displaying his considerable wealth! When the Prince declared that all good Royalist supporters were giving their plate to the King as war contributions, he almost fainted, he turned so pale! There was nought he could do but offer his to the Prince, but it was clear that it pained him enormously!"

"He gave all the plate to the Prince?" Drusilla asked in astonishment.

"Aye, if reluctantly, and Rupert had it carried off immediately before he could change his mind!"

"It was not his to give!" Drusilla

exclaimed. "How dare the Prince? Oh, this is yet another example of the endless exactions we are subject to! Is it not enough to expect us to support the army, and contribute towards the King's expenses, and tax my brother three times what others have to pay simply because he went on that wretched deputation to Parliament, so that he is forced to flee, leaving Elizabeth and myself at the mercy of any who choose to impose on us? Must our plate be stolen, too?"

"Wait, I do not understand. How was it not the Mayor's? Did it belong to the town, is that it?"

"No, though that would have been as bad. The Mayor, fool that he is, wished to impress, and so he borrowed plate from all who would lend it."

Sir Randal gave a shout of laughter.

"He was asked if it was his, and said that it was," he explained. "No matter, he must make his own excuses to the owners of it. They may consider that it has been put to a good cause. What is this of your brother?"

Drusilla explained the triple tax that had been imposed on James.

"With the result," she concluded bitterly, "that whether he wished it or no he has been driven to throw in his lot with the Parliamentary army. Elizabeth is ill with worry!"

"I am sorry. Is there aught I can do? Have soldiers been billeted on you this time?"

Drusilla struggled hard to prevent herself from falling under the spell of his charm. The unknown Percy cousin had to be fiercely dredged from the recesses of her mind, but she succeeded, and answered curtly.

"Thank you, but no. My sister-in-law has been more fortunate this time, and in consideration of her health the Governor placed with us one of his own men and his wife. They are very quiet and we see nought of them apart from at mealtimes."

"May I call on Mistress Matthews?"

"If you wish, Sir Randal. Now I beg you to excuse me. I have lingered overlong and must return home."

Puzzled by her aloofness, Sir Randal permitted her to depart and watched her walk quickly away, a frown in his eyes.

Had the exactions of the King caused this change in Drusilla? He had been fully convinced when he was last in Reading that she was as attracted to him as he was to her. Did she blame him for the heavy taxation on her brother? Or for the stupid misunderstanding that had led to the Prince commandeering the plate belonging to citizens other than the Mayor? Somehow he did not think either would have been sufficient to cause such a change, and he determined to discover as soon as possible what ailed her.

Accordingly he waited near her house on the following morning until he saw her leave, a shopping basket over her arm, and then presented himself to Elizabeth.

"Sir Randal! I had no notion that you were in Reading! Do you mean to stay long?"

"I must return to Oxford shortly," he replied, noting that Drusilla for some reason had not disclosed his presence. "How is Mistress Drusilla?"

Elizabeth gave him a sharp glance.

"She is well, and will be sorry to have missed you. She is to marry Mr Blagrave in June, you know," she added brightly.

"An excellent match for her, as she realises."

So that was it, Randal thought. Had Drusilla, unlikely as it seemed, willingly accepted this match, or was she being in some way constrained? At all events it seemed clear now why she had been so cold to him. After some further general conversation he took his leave, begging Elizabeth to give his regards to Drusilla, and planning ways in which he could contrive to meet her alone.

He did not believe that she could love Jacob Blagrave. Her manner towards him only a few weeks previously had been anything but friendly, and he wondered what pressures had been brought to bear on Drusilla to cause her to consent to such a match, suitable though it might appear from a worldly point of view.

Drusilla had been able to compose herself and decide on her course of action when Randal waylaid her by the fortifications on the following morning. Determined not to permit him to see what she felt for him, since she was convinced he was merely amusing himself with a flirtation, she was coldly polite, and would have refused his offered company had she not been some distance from home, and clearly on her way there.

"I understand that you are to be congratulated," he said without preamble. "Jacob Blagrave is a fortunate man, but when I last saw you I would not have thought him the man to win your heart."

She glanced up at him, shaken at this direct attack, and then quickly veiled her eyes.

"Marriage is a business," she said calmly, "by which men and women gain advancement for their families and themselves. Do you not agree?"

"Oddly enough I do not. Do you?" he demanded.

She shrugged.

"I think that any other way leads to disillusion and misery. Surely it is better to expect little and be satisfied with it, rather than strive for the unattainable?" she asked, unable to fully hide the bleakness of her tone.

They were passing through the Abbey ruins, which were for the moment deserted. Randal took Drusilla's arm and pulled her round to face him, drawing her into a secluded niche between two half broken walls.

"My dear, you must not! You do not love the man! Why have you agreed to marry with such a one, when you are made for love! That way lies misery and disillusion! Are you being forced? Is it your parents or your brother? What hold has Blagrave over you?"

He was gripping her arms fiercely, but Drusilla did not heed the pain. She was concentrating all her will on the effort not to tell him that he was wrong, that she would never marry Jacob Blagrave, that she wanted to marry for love. He must not see how she felt, for it would be too humiliating to become just one more conquest that had amused the gallant Sir Randal for a few idle hours.

"You have no right to question me!" she gasped. "I am not being compelled in any way!"

Suddenly Randal released her arms, only to pull her into a close embrace. Drusilla closed her eyes as his lips, hard and demanding, came down on hers, and she was crushed to him. For a few moments she revelled in the bliss of it, and her response was enough to satisfy Randal that he had not mistaken her feelings for him. Then, as Drusilla realised what was happening, she began to struggle, and he immediately released her but caught hold of her hands in one of his, and with the other forced her to turn her face up to him.

"Can you swear that you intend to marry Blagrave?" he demanded.

"Would you have me called fickle as well as too difficult to please?" she cried wildly. "Love — is — not in question! Oh, pray release me!"

"Where is your brother?" he asked abruptly.

"I do not know! Somewhere with the Parliamentary army, but we have had no news! What is it to you?"

Randal smiled, and hugged her to him briefly.

"Come, I will see you home."

They walked in silence until a few yards away from her home, Randal spoke softly to Drusilla.

"Do not fear, I will return, my love," he promised, and was gone.

4

THE next few months were agony for Drusilla. She had seen no more of Sir Randal who had departed for Oxford and she wavered between hope that his kisses and his parting promise had been more than mere flirtation, and bitter apprehension that she was cruelly deceiving herself. A further letter from Mistress Rogers coupling the names of Mary Percy and Sir Randal, and declaring that she had it straight from his sister that a betrothal was imminent threw her into a black despair.

Elizabeth became more and more lethargic and absorbed in the coming baby as her pregnancy advanced, and showed interest in public events only when the occasional letter from James arrived. He had joined Sir William Waller, who in December had captured Winchester. By February, Waller had been sent to Gloucestershire, and James wrote that he had been able to make a brief visit to his parents on the way. He wrote that although the severe weather at the end of January had caused the loss of many sheep, his parents were well. They were looking forward to visiting Elizabeth with her new baby, and seeing Drusilla married, in a few months.

The fines and assessments and building of fortifications went on, but Drusilla scarcely cared. Even when all the wool was impounded and the bales used for the defences she made but slight protest. She watched listlessly as the cannon brought from Oxford were set in position in the Market Place, Friar Street, and Broad Street, even at the top of the church tower, and did not comment when Jacob came to report that the King desired the clothiers to continue trading with London, and advised them to ask the permission of Parliament.

In the middle of February there was some excitement at the rumours that Essex was moving against the town, but it came to nought, for instead he drove the Royalists out of Henley. Then he moved towards Oxford and the citizens breathed sighs of relief, believing that he had passed them by. Drusilla first heard that these hopes had been premature when Meg, who was thoroughly enjoying herself with so many soldiers stationed in the town, ran in to report that one of her trooper friends had returned from a scouting party with the news that Lord Essex had swung southwards again and his army was approaching Reading through Wargrave and Binfield Heath.

"They'll march straight in, Mistress Drusilla!" she cried in fear. "There's no good defences, Jonah says. Why, even the townsmen who joined the new regiment are deserting faster than they joined!"

"You know well that is because they were impressed, and further, received no pay!" Drusilla said. "Be sensible, Meg, they are not here yet!"

"They soon will be, and then what will become of us?"

"What should, with my brother in the Parliament's army? I pray you, Meg, not to show your fears to your mistress, for if she is frightened the worst could happen!"

Meg, thus reminded of Elizabeth's condition, succeeded in remaining outwardly calm, and Elizabeth herself showed no fear, for she fully expected that James would soon be with her if the news were true.

On Saturday, April the fifteenth, the people of Reading found themselves facing that for which the Royalists had been preparing all winter when Lord Essex and his men finally appeared before the town.

Jacob Blagrave, having been busy during the winter in forwarding himself in the eyes of the Royalists, was in a quandary. He dared support neither side without positive guidance as to the outcome of the struggle, and in consequence was peevish and fretful when he made a visit to Drusilla.

"I cannot think it wise of Sir Arthur to have refused to send out the women and children," he complained. "Lord Essex offered him the opportunity, but he refused. It would have meant more stocks of food for the defenders," he added, "and I fear that if the siege lasts more than a few weeks we shall grow very short of food!"

"How terrible for you," Drusilla said

scornfully. "I collect there would have been ample food for the women and children, supplied by the generosity of Lord Essex to his enemies, had we been pushed out of the town defenceless? Where would we have found shelter? In the army tents down in the river meadows? Or in Caversham Church? I believe there is still some of it standing after Lord Essex attacked it!"

"You choose to jest!" Jacob said angrily, "but apart from lack of food, there will soon be a lack of powder! It is useless resisting! It will only make the reprisals greater when they do get in!"

"Not for those who show that they are only too ready to welcome whoever is victorious!" Drusilla said acidly, and to her relief Jacob soon went away, saying that he wished to see whether there were more besiegers to the north-east, for as yet he had news of only one regiment encamped there.

"A pity he does not take the opportunity to flee then!" Drusilla commented.

Throughout the winter Jacob had blithely assumed that he and Drusilla were firmly betrothed, and although, with James being away, she had been spared the embarrassment of having to deny a definite announcement, she found that the news was generally known, and that her angry denials of it were regarded either as girlish confusion, or by the more charitable, as useless attempts to maintain some propriety while her brother was not on hand to make the conventional communication.

She had ceased to argue with Jacob, contenting herself with repeated refusals to discuss the matter, since she would never consent. He was immune to this treatment, and Drusilla bore his complacency as well as she could, sometimes thinking that it would in reality be easier to give up the struggle and permit her family to dispose of her as they chose. A small inner voice always made itself heard, though, with the question of what would then happen if Sir Randal returned, as he had promised, and though she tried to suppress the hope she never succeeded it totally killing it.

Sunday and Monday passed, with no real attack by the besiegers. It was reported that they were gathering more troops about the town, but they did no more than fire desultorily on the defenders, so that the townsfolk summoned up the courage to go to the ramparts and gaze over them at the novel sight of cannon in the meadows pointing at them, and beyond these strings of white tents fringing the river.

Meg, stealing away from the house early on Tuesday morning on the pretence of shopping, came running back in tremendous excitement a few minutes later.

"Mistress Drusilla!" she gasped, finding her in the kitchen. "Come and see! Do come!"

"What in the world is it?"

"Barges, Mistress, that have come up the river during the night, right past the soldiers, and brought us more powder, they say!"

"Come right past? How is that?"

"I cannot tell, but do let us go and discover what we can!"

Knowing that Elizabeth was resting, Drusilla gave Joan and the cook swift instructions as she untied her apron and swiftly smoothed her hair, then shook out the skirt of the green and white striped gown she was wearing. Bidding them not to leave the house, she ran with Meg to where an excited crowd of citizens had gathered to greet these daring Royalists, who had conveyed the barges from Sonning right under the noses of the Parliamentarians and into the centre of the town. Many musketeers had also come to augment the defending forces, and they brought the news that the King would soon be marching to the relief of Reading.

Drusilla was listening to an account of this, gazing wonderingly at the barges, when she gasped with shock. On the last barge a familiar figure was talking with a small group of men and the Governor, Sir Arthur Aston. As she watched, scarcely able to believe her eyes, Sir Randal turned, saw her, and waved his hand in greeting. He speedily concluded his conversation with the others and walked across to Drusilla.

"I have duties to attend to now, but I will come to you later," he said swiftly, and with a bow was gone.

In a dream Drusilla walked home, and

was able to concentrate on nothing for the rest of the day. Her thoughts were in a turmoil. Had Sir Randal's arrival been mere coincidence, or had he deliberately come into the threatened town because of her? Did he wish just to carry on an agreeable flirtation, or were his feelings for her deeper than that? To voluntarily enter a besieged town seemed somewhat extreme if his motive was nought but flirtation, and yet, as a soldier, he might have been simply obeying orders, and his appearance be in no way connected with her. For whole minutes at a time she permitted herself to hope, then chided herself with being unrealistic. As the day wore on and he did not appear she began to wonder if she had imagined the whole, until, at suppertime, there was a knock on the door, and her heart began to beat wildly.

"Mr Blagrave, Ma'am," Meg announced, and Drusilla could have cried with annoyance and frustration.

"Mr Blagrave, is aught amiss?" Elizabeth asked in alarm.

"No, dear Mistress Matthews. Forgive me for calling so late, but I thought that you might have heard rumours and been alarmed."

"We have heard of nought but the arrival of the barges," Elizabeth replied, "and as Drusilla saw them they are not rumour."

"It has been an eventful day."

He sat down on Elizabeth's invitation and accepted a glass of wine.

"First the barges," he said slowly, "then for some reason, despite the reinforcements, Sir Arthur offered to surrender if he were allowed to march out with his men and baggage."

"What? And leave us to the mercy of Lord Essex?" Drusilla exclaimed.

"I thought you maintained that he would do you no harm?" Jacob asked, and Drusilla shrugged. She did not know what to think. "But Lord Essex refused, saying that he wanted the men. One cannot help wondering whether some message, some news of the King, came in by the barges which either made it advantageous for Sir Arthur to leave, or to make it appear so. However, he will make no more such decisions."

"Why so? Has he been killed? We

93

heard the firing all day, but had become used to it!"

"Not killed, but struck dumb from being hit on the head with a falling tile, and Colonel Richard Fielding is now in charge. I do not know how we shall fare with him. He ordered a sally, but it was repulsed and Essex has drawn nearer. He has more reinforcements, and I am told Sir William Waller has sent men from the west."

"Then James may be there! Oh, how soon will it take them to capture the town?" Elizabeth asked.

Drusilla experienced a moment of panic. If the town fell Sir Randal might be taken prisoner, or even worse, killed, but if the Royalists were victorious James was in equal danger.

She had no time for further consideration, for Meg again appeared, followed by Sir Randal, and Elizabeth, who had not known that he was in the town, exclaimed in surprise and demanded to know how he had contrived to enter it. Jacob was staring at the newcomer with undisguised hostility while Drusilla, after one joyous glance, kept her head lowered and her eyes veiled for fear that everyone should see the delight in them.

"I came with the advance troops, Ma'am," Sir Randal was explaining. "The King marches from Oxford with Prince Rupert and will soon be here. But how have you fared since last I saw you? Have you news of your husband?"

"He has been with Sir William Waller, who is now, I am told, outside the town!"

"So I, too, have heard. Well, Mistress Matthews, although he and I are on opposing sides, I hope that you will soon be reunited with him. If Essex is victorious then it will be easy, but if matters are settled differently I will do what I can to secure a pass for him to enable him to visit you."

He did not stay long, saying that there was much to be done, but that he would come to enquire after them on the following day. To Drusilla's surprise, Jacob rose to depart with him, saying that he would walk with Sir Randal part of the way.

The men left and walked in silence for a while, Sir Randal surveying his companion in some amusement, for he was obviously labouring under the stress of some deep emotion. At last Jacob halted and took a deep breath.

"A moment, if you please!" he jerked out.

Sir Randal leaned negligently against a convenient wall, his eyebrows raised interrogatively.

"I would have you know that Mistress Drusilla and I are betrothed," Jacob said in something of a rush. "I do not permit other men to trifle with her and so, Sir Randal, I ask you to cease your visits to her, and your attempts to curry favour with Mistress Matthews by such ploys as offering passes that you know well you will never be in a position to procure!"

"You may be under the impression that Mistress Drusilla is betrothed to you," Sir Randal drawled, "but that is a long way from marriage, especially in these uncertain times!"

"Do you threaten me?" Jacob blustered. "I demand satisfaction!"

Sir Randal burst out laughing.

"Pray do not be such a fool!"

"Fool! You call me a fool? You shall

pay for that! Who are your friends?"

"I have many friends," Sir Randal said, laughing, "but none whom I would insult by asking them to support me over such a ridiculous matter with such as you! I do not fight unmannerly boys with imagined grievances, and so, Mr Blagrave, I will bid you goodnight!"

He straightened, about to move away, and Jacob, spurred on to action by the contempt in his voice, flung the glove he had been nervously clutching into Sir Randal's face. Sir Randal, moving lightly and rapidly, sidestepped the blow and turned so that he was facing Jacob.

"You need a lesson, you young booby," he said quietly. "Put up your fists!"

Jacob, filled with vainglorious ideas of vanquishing Sir Randal by the superior method of swordplay, did not at all care for this turn of events. He backed hastily away.

"I have challenged you!" he gasped.

"You have insulted me, and I do not accept challenges from impertinent boys, I teach them manners!"

So saying he moved forward, and brushing aside with contemptuous ease

Jacob's reluctantly raised guard, floored him with a light but precisely delivered blow to the chin. As Jacob writhed on the ground, prudence overcoming his rage and humiliation and dictating that he did not give way to his desire to resume battle, Sir Randal surveyed him dispassionately.

"Next time I will cast you in the river to dampen your temper," he warned, and turned, leaving Jacob to recover the shreds of his dignity alone, thankful that he had chosen a deserted spot for his abortive attempt at forcing a duel on his rival, and already weaving schemes of vengeance.

Mr Blagrave did not visit Drusilla on the following day, during which the bombardment continued so that the church of St Giles was damaged so severely that the cannon in the tower had to be brought down, but Sir Randal came after dark, saying that he could not stay long but wished to be told if there was aught he could do.

He was leaving and had just stepped out of the door when from an alleyway opposite four men with knives and clubs attacked him. Randal had just time to draw his sword and back against the wall of the house before they were on to him. Meg, who had not closed the front door, screamed in terror, and Drusilla, followed by Elizabeth, ran out of the parlour to discover what was amiss.

Defending himself with his sword, Randal was keeping the men at bay, but as she watched, aghast, one of them contrived to swing his club and get through Randal's guard, bringing the heavy club down on his left shoulder. Randal winced with pain, but did not allow his concentration to falter, and slashed out, cutting the tendons of one ruffian's arm so that he dropped his weapons and retired from the fight, howling in agony.

"Come back into the house!" Drusilla cried, but it appeared that Sir Randal was attempting to move away from the refuge of the door.

In this he was unsuccessful, for one of the bullies was creeping along the wall at the far side, hugging it closely, and forcing Sir Randal backwards. In the confined space and with the two others to deal with also he could not use his sword to advantage. He did disarm another of the men, who collapsed, moaning and clutching his leg which the sword had cut open, but at the same moment one of the others threw a cloak, and Sir Randal, in leaping backwards in a vain attempt to prevent his sword from becoming entangled in it, was almost by the door.

Meg, with a scream, fled back towards the kitchen regions as the two remaining attackers rushed on Sir Randal and bore him and a fiercely resisting Drusilla back into the house.

They swept past her, leaving her clinging to the doorpost, and she saw that one of them had Sir Randal's sword arm in a fierce grip, while the other was on the point of bringing down his cudgel on Sir Randal's head. Not stopping to think she flung herself forward and seized his arm so that the blow was deflected. In the brief respite Sir Randal wrenched himself free and sank his dagger deep into the body of the man who had been holding him, then turned to face the last opponent, who had retreated to the stairs and stood a little way up them, a knife ready in one hand and his cudgel in the other. Sir Randal started towards him, and taking careful aim, the villain threw the knife straight at Sir Randal, and leapt down in expectation of finishing him off with a blow from the cudgel.

Sir Randal, however, had anticipated the attack and swerved to avoid the knife, at the same time springing forward so that the man, unable to halt the impetus of his forward movement, fell with a groan on to Sir Randal's sword.

Dragging his sword free and wiping the blood from it, Sir Randal surveyed the bodies of the two men he had killed.

"Thank you for your timely assistance," he murmured, glancing with a crooked smile at Drusilla, and then his expression changed and he stepped hastily over to the doorway of the parlour. Looking round, Drusilla, somewhat dazed, saw the crumpled figure of Elizabeth lying in the doorway where, unnoticed, she had collapsed in a swoon.

"I will carry her to her bed. Summon the maids," he ordered briskly, and Drusilla fled to the kitchen where Meg and Joan, with the cook and Willy, the groom, were cowering at the far side of the table.

"Quickly, the mistress has fainted. Go to her, Meg. I must fetch the midwife!"

They gaped at her, then Joan, quicker-witted than the rest, seized a bowl and filled it from the kettle hanging above the fire.

"Send Willy," she suggested, but Drusilla shook her head distractedly.

"No, for there may be more of those scum outside waiting. They will not attack me, and I will go by back ways. Go and do what Sir Randal tells you!"

"Is — is he hurt, Mistress?" quavered Meg, but Drusilla did not wait to reply, running out of the back door and across to the gate near the stables which led into a side road.

All was peaceful outside, and she soon reached the house of the old woman who acted as midwife.

"I fear my sister-in-law will miscarry after the shock," she gasped breathlessly, but the old woman, fuddled with drink and warmth after an arduous night and day attending a difficult delivery, did not wish to be dragged from her comfort.

"Pooh, nonsense! She was healthy when I saw her last week. She's past the danger of miscarriages, unlike the other times, and will soon recover from a swoon. It's common in her state, for she's too much sensibility. Now let me be!"

None of Drusilla's entreaties could move her, and at last she was forced to return home, praying desperately that the old woman was right and that no harm could come to Elizabeth.

Her hopes were misplaced, for she found when she ran back into the kitchen that Willy was distractedly busy boiling cauldrons of water and carrying them up to Elizabeth's room. Running before him, she met Randal at the door and he took her hands in his.

"She is in labour. Where is the midwife?"

"She would not come! She was drunk! What shall we do?"

"You can help most by trying to sooth her. I'll fetch the garrison surgeon. Is there no other midwife?"

"No!"

"Some older friend, with children of her own?"

"Mistress Tanner, our neighbour, has a large family, but as she is so much older we have never seen much of her. She seems kind, and would most likely help."

"Send Willy for her. I'll go to the garrison, but I'll return very soon."

"They might attack you again!" she protested.

"No, no, for we accounted for them all," he reassured her, but humoured her to the extent of agreeing to leave by the back door.

Elizabeth was stretched on the bed, her hands clenched and her face pale. As Drusilla tiptoed across to her a spasm of pain gripped her and she cried out in agony.

The next few hours were ever afterwards a blur to Drusilla. She had an impression of Elizabeth writhing in agony, and screaming unbearably, while a tall dark man and Mistress Tanner conferred in worried whispers, and the servants hovered anxiously by the door, speeding off to execute the surgeon's commands or fetch what he requested. The words 'too soon' and 'badly positioned' echoed constantly in her brain, and she remembered resisting Sir Randal at first, so that he ignored her protests and picked her up to carry her from the room and downstairs where he forced her to take a glass of wine, restoring her senses somewhat.

It was not until half way through the following day that Elizabeth gave birth to a shrivelled, stillborn infant who would have been the son she and James had longed for. The midwife, having thought better of her refusal the previous night, appeared midway through the morning and was sent packing with a few blistering words from Sir Randal. Having done all he could, the surgeon left Elizabeth in Mistress Tanner's charge and ordered Drusilla to bed, giving her a sleeping draught and promising to come back in the evening to see how they did.

Drusilla awakened at nightfall, to find Elizabeth tossing in a delirious fever, and Mistress Tanner seriously concerned.

"She had not the strength for such an ordeal," she said quietly.

"You must need rest yourself," Drusilla responded, "for you have been with her all last night and today. Tell me what to do and I will sit with her now. Thank you for — for — " she broke off, wiping away her tears, and Mistress Tanner tried to comfort her.

"There, there, little one! This often happens, fever after the birth, and we must not expect the worst! Promise that you will send for me if there is any change? If you promise that, I will go home now."

Drusilla dried her eyes and tried to smile.

"I will do so, for I could not manage without you," she said.

"Good. The surgeon is to come soon, and no doubt Sir Randal will be here again. He has called almost every hour since you were put to bed."

For the first time Drusilla recalled the fight that had been the cause of Elizabeth's swoon.

"What did he do with — with those men?" she asked hesitantly, but Mistress Tanner knew nothing, looking puzzled, and Drusilla learned later from Joan that Sir Randal had thrown the bodies into the street while she herself was fetching the midwife, and had afterwards brought back some soldiers as well as the surgeon and had them removed.

"Willy says he recognised one of them, a tailor who works for Mr Daniel Blagrave."

"The town councillor?" Drusilla commented. And Jacob Blagrave's cousin, she added silently, a horrible suspicion forming in her mind.

"And Meg saw Anne Butcher today, and discovered that her brother Ben, who's always getting drunk and into brawls, has a cut arm. Didn't Sir Randal almost chop the arm off one of them?" Joan asked ghoulishly, and Drusilla shuddered.

"Has — has Mr Blagrave called today?" she asked, and was told that he had not been seen.

She had little time for further reflection, however, for all her attention was taken with nursing Elizabeth. Meg came in with the news that the besiegers had moved closer, and had caught and hanged a deserter who had been in the process of blowing up their ammunition train, but Drusilla scarcely listened. She sat with Elizabeth all night, and rested for a few hours when Mistress Tanner returned and firmly told her that she would do Elizabeth no good by making herself ill.

When Sir Randal came she refused to walk out with him, saying that she dared not be long away from Elizabeth. On the following day, however, Elizabeth's fever seemed to have subsided, and Mistress Tanner's exhortations, coupled with Sir Randal's persuasions, made her consent to take the air for a short while.

As they walked towards the river, Drusilla did not speak apart from repeating her thanks for the help Sir Randal had given, but after a time, when his silent sympathy had calmed and somewhat restored her spirits, she asked whether he had any notion of who might have attacked him, and why.

"I have a suspicion," he replied. "Do you know aught?"

She told him what she had heard, and he nodded.

"We took the bodies away, but they have not been claimed. I hope still to identify them. We searched for the two I wounded, but they had been able to get away. I think I'll visit this fellow Butcher. He might be willing to loosen his tongue, for gold or threats!"

He did not reveal to her his encounter

with Jacob Blagrave, but tried to distract her thoughts by telling her of the bravery of a man named Flower, a servant of Sir Lucius Dives, who had swum across the swollen river to bring news that the King was on his way to the relief of the town.

"We shall soon see the last of them," he promised, indicating the army encampment below where they stood, on the Forbury ramparts.

For the next two days, however, nothing seemed to change. There was no further news of the King's approach, and no major assault on the town. Elizabeth lay in a state of drowsiness, from which she roused with occasional lucid intervals, and Jacob Blagrave, uncharacteristically, did not visit them until the morning of Tuesday, the twenty-fifth. Hoping to discover whether her suspicions were correct, Drusilla consented to see him and descended to the parlour.

"My dear!" he greeted her, and moved forwards, his hands outstretched.

She evaded him and sat down.

"I cannot leave my sister for long."

"No, of course not. I came to commiserate

109

with you, and see how she does."

"The same," Drusilla replied. "I have been surprised not to have seen you since the night it happened. One of your cousin Daniel's men was involved," she said bluntly.

"What is that you say?" he said in a puzzled tone, but his eyes evaded hers.

"One of the men who tried to murder Sir Randal in this house was recognised as a tailor who worked for your cousin," she stated calmly.

"And from that you blame me? Well, that is beyond a jest!" he blustered.

"It is no jest that Elizabeth was caused to lose her baby, and possibly her own life," Drusilla retorted.

Jacob had recovered himself.

"Of course not. I merely meant that in these days one can have little knowledge of, or control over, the men one employs."

"No, indeed, for they all make mistakes, do they not?" Drusilla agreed coldly.

Jacob nodded and changed the subject.

"Had you heard that the Governor asks for a parley? He has been flying the white flags since early this morning."

"But — where is the King? I thought

he was coming!" Drusilla exclaimed in dismay.

"It seems that he has been defeated. Hostages have been exchanged, and the Corporation are meeting at this very minute. They will be in a great puzzle to know what to do!"

"Have you made up your mind?" she asked, momentarily diverted.

Before he could reply, they heard the sound of firing coming from the north, and as they looked up, startled, running feet pounded along the street outside. Drusilla ran to the window, opened it and leaned out, while Jacob begged her to take care.

"What is it?" she cried, and one of the pikemen running past gave her a cheery wave.

"The King is here!" he called. "He's behind Essex and attacking Caversham Bridge. We'll soon show those Parliamentary rebels how to fight!"

5

JACOB immediately announced that he must go to discover the truth of this latest rumour, and Drusilla would have gone with him had Elizabeth not just then called out to her.

For the whole of that day Elizabeth grew worse, relapsing again into delirium, and so restless that Drusilla could scarcely leave her to snatch an hour or two on her own bed. Meg and Jacob brought news, but Drusilla was too worried about Elizabeth's condition to take much of it in. The King's attack had been halted, thanks partly to a fierce hail storm, and the King's forces had withdrawn to Caversham Church. Colonel Fielding was to be permitted to cross the lines and confer with the King, and terms would be agreed with Essex.

"The Royalists are about to leave!" Jacob stated with a gleam in his eye when he came and saw Drusilla briefly on the Wednesday evening.

112

She hardly cared, for Elizabeth was now so weak that there seemed no hope for her. Even when Drusilla tried to rally her by saying that James would be there on the following day, Elizabeth's eyelids barely flickered in acknowledgement. The surgeon, with a respite from his garrison duties during the truce, shook his head and told Drusilla that he doubted whether she would last the night. Mistress Tanner joined Drusilla in their last sad vigil, and before midnight Elizabeth breathed her last.

Spent with grief, Drusilla allowed Mistress Tanner to tuck her up in bed, and slept heavily. When she awoke, Joan was sitting beside her bed and, her own eyes full of tears, said that she had orders to see that Drusilla remained there for a while. She helped Drusilla brush out her curls, saying that she would feel more the thing when she had eaten, and went to fetch a tray with a bowl of chicken broth. To her surprise, Drusilla did feel better, and insisted on getting up.

"There is so much to be done," she

said slowly, as she pulled on a sober grey gown.

"Well, Mistress Tanner and — and — we have done a great deal!" Joan stammered.

Drusilla looked at her, puzzled, but was too weary to probe into this strange remark. She went downstairs, and hearing voices in the parlour, opened the door and looked in. Mistress Tanner and Sir Randal were sitting there talking quietly. Sir Randal rose immediately and came to take her hand and draw her to a chair beside the fire.

"Sit down, there is much to discuss," he said quietly.

"How — do you come here?" Drusilla asked, frowning. "I — what is happening? I thought the siege was over? Did not someone say that you were leaving?"

"Yes," he replied curtly. "We leave tomorrow, and that is why I am here. I want you to come with me."

Drusilla looked at him blankly.

"But Elizabeth? I cannot leave her — like that!"

Mistress Tanner came across and took Drusilla's hand.

"No, my dear, and that is why Sir Randal and I — Sir Randal came last night, you see, just after you had gone to bed — why we have taken it upon ourselves to speed up the arrangements for the burial. I laid out your sister-in-law's body early this morning, and she is to be buried in an hour's time, before the garrison leaves."

"So soon? But if you leave," she said, turning to Randal, "does that not mean that the Parliamentary army will enter? James might be there! He would never forgive me if I had Elizabeth buried in so much haste, and he had no last opportunity to make his farewells!"

"James is unlikely to be there, Drusilla. It was merely a rumour that some of Waller's troops were at the siege. He is still on the Welsh borders, and James, too. It will be weeks before James can be told and return to Reading. In the meantime you will be alone here, and at the mercy of the Parliamentary troops. I propose to take you to Devizes, to your parents."

"I cannot like it, sending you away so," Mistress Tanner said worriedly, "but it is the only safe plan."

"And leave James' house and business for Parliament to plunder?" Drusilla said sharply.

"They are his friends."

"Do you truly believe that they will show respect for it, Sir Randal?"

"No, neither do I believe they will show respect for you," he said bluntly. "You could not prevent them doing what they chose, and so you must consider your own safety."

"No, I will not run away."

They pleaded and argued with her, but Drusilla would not move from her stance. Someone must protect James' property, and if there were no one else, she would have to do it.

"He has lost Elizabeth, would you have me throw away all else?"

Randal suddenly gave way, and he and Mistress Tanner left for a while to prepare the final arrangements for the burial. Later Mistress Tanner returned to sit with Drusilla when Elizabeth's body was taken to the churchyard, accompanied by only a few of James' neighbours and business associates who, in the bustle and confusion of the ending of the siege, had heard of her death and came to pay their last respects.

Randal came back afterwards to make his farewells, and to return, with a smile, the pistols which had been the cause of his first meeting with Drusilla. When he again asked her to leave with him she was desperately torn, for she knew that it was most unlikely that she would ever see him again, but she shook her head, repeating that she must protect James' house, and watched bleakly as he finally left the room.

Mistress Tanner remained, and her talk of Elizabeth appeared to soothe Drusilla, who had refused either to eat any supper or to retire to bed. In an odd way, thinking of Elizabeth eased the pain she felt at the departure of Sir Randal. It was late in the evening when Mr Blagrave's voice, raised in anger, was heard at the front door.

"Announce me, girl! I have a better right than any to be with your mistress at such a time!"

"She's not fit to see visitors," Meg's high, indignant tones could be heard as she protested vigorously, but she was rudely thrust out of the way and Jacob entered the parlour unceremoniously, to glare about him suspiciously before he advanced to take Drusilla's hand.

"My dear, I have but this moment heard! I have been with my cousin most of the day, preparing for the entry of the Parliamentary army tomorrow, and it was only when Dr Wilde came to us that I heard of the tragic death of Mistress Matthews."

Drusilla shrank from his loud voice, and tried to withdraw her hand, but he held it tightly, and began to pat it as he talked.

"Naturally I would have been here to support you had I known, and would have aided you in the arrangements. Why did you not send for me? I would have advised you, and I cannot think that whoever urged you to so hasty a burial did right," he added, shooting a glance of dislike at Mistress Tanner. "However, I am here now, and you need turn to no one else for help. I heard," he said bitterly, "that the fellow who has been making such a nuisance of himself has been here, interfering in what was none of his business."

"If you mean Sir Randal Thornton," Drusilla declared, two bright spots of colour appearing in her cheeks, and her spirits roused by this unjust attack, "indeed he has been here, and most considerate and helpful he has been! And pray release my hand, Mr Blagrave!"

She succeeded in snatching her hand away, but Jacob, undeterred, seated himself beside her on the settle.

"He was scarcely the right person to turn to," he commented. "After all, he has no connection with the family."

"And neither do you, and you will not have!" Drusilla cried.

"Oh, my dear, you speak hastily because you are distraught. It has all been settled these six months past. No doubt, with all there is to be done, and because of Elizabeth's death, naturally, our wedding will have to be delayed a while, but as soon as James returns we will arrange it."

Drusilla almost stamped her foot with rage.

"Understand me, Jacob Blagrave, I have

never contemplated or agreed to any marriage with you, and I never will! If you have no more sense or consideration than to come worrying me with your unwelcome attentions almost before my sister is cold, then it is time you learned! I hate and detest you, do you understand? You are the last man I would ever marry, and I wish that you would go away and stay away," she concluded, and promptly burst into tears.

Mistress Tanner came swiftly across the room and took the weeping girl into her arms.

"Pray leave us, Mr Blagrave," she said coldly, but he shook his head.

"Drusilla is overwrought, indeed, and upset by the interference of strangers. I have urgent matters to discuss with her, and when she is a little calmer, as no doubt, being a well-conducted female normally, she soon will be, we can talk seriously. You need have no qualms about leaving us alone together for a while, Mistress Tanner, when you have soothed her, for we are a betrothed couple."

Mistress Tanner looked at him in utter amazement, and fearing that Drusilla would fly out at him and attack him physically, as, she afterwards confided to her spouse, she had very nearly done herself, she manoeuvred herself and the girl out of the room to find Meg, still bursting with annoyance at having been forced to admit him, standing in the hall.

Carefully Mistress Tanner shut the door.

"Leave him to cool his head for ten minutes or so, and then tell him Mistress Drusilla has gone to bed and is asleep," she said, and as Meg nodded, led an unprotesting Drusilla upstairs.

"I must go home for a while, my dear, when we are sure that he has gone, but I will come back and sleep here. I do not care to leave you alone with none but servants."

"You are kind to me!" Drusilla whispered. "Pray make him go!"

"You may be sure I will, if I have to send for the constable! Although he's been spreading it about the town, I had an idea that you did not want the match, and after tonight I am not surprised. Of all the senseless, pompous fools!"

"James wants it," Drusilla said listlessly.

"H'm. Then he's no more sense than a bantam, though I shouldn't be saying so to you!"

Drusilla smiled faintly.

"He does not regard it that I detest Mr Blagrave!"

"No wonder you do, if his behaviour is often so foolish. Sir Randal is so totally different, is he not?"

Drusilla bit her lip, suddenly recalling that Sir Randal would have left Reading by the following morning, and that she was unlikely ever to see him again, then turned to bury her face in the pillows. Mistress Tanner, smiling at this confirmation of her own suspicions, whispered goodnight and blew out the candle, then went downstairs to learn from Meg that a disgruntled Mr Blagrave had taken himself off, saying that he would return in the morning.

"That he will not!" Mistress Tanner declared. "I'll bring my husband's man, Ned, to answer the door. No Jacob Blagrave will force his way past him!"

This ploy succeeded, and Drusilla was left in peace. Meg had been out to

122

wave goodbye to her soldier friends as they marched out, and she was full of the news.

"The Governor, Sir Arthur, was carried out first, poor man. Fancy, he has not spoken since he was hit on the head by that tile! He was carried in a scarlet horse litter, lined with white. I wonder if the Queen has one so grand? After him went the coaches and wagons, and then the troopers and dragoons. My, it was a brave sight, to see them march so proudly, drums beating and trumpets sounding, and the soldiers following, carrying their colours."

"Did you see Sir Randal?" Drusilla could not forbear to ask.

"No, Mistress, but I was too far away to recognise one man."

"Have the Parliamentary troops come into the town?" Mistress Tanner asked.

"Aye, they almost passed one another at Friar's Corner. But before that there was some sort of scuffle on the far side of the river. It looked as though the Royalists were being attacked, but it was not for long. I was told that their officers stopped it."

"Let us hope that they are as successful at preventing disorder within the town."

"For sure it will be fine, Mistress Tanner," Meg replied blithely. "I hear they have all been promised twelve whole shillings instead of plunder so we shall not have trouble."

Her confidence was misplaced, for soon loud shouts and the sound of singing could be heard in the streets. Drusilla, fearful, ordered the doors and windows to be barred, and stationed herself, armed with a large carving knife, at a front upstairs window from where she could see what went on. She insisted on having her dinner on a tray there, saying that she dared not leave, and soon afterwards her fears were confirmed when a band of riotous infantry, brandishing sticks and swords and whatever weapons they could find, turned into the street. They began, systematically, to break into the houses on the far side, dragging out the frightened inhabitants, carrying off valuables and any other goods that took their fancy.

One man, wearing a tasselled nightcap, was gnawing at a leg of chicken when a terrified girl, a maid Drusilla recognised as coming from the apothecary's house, tried to run out of the house and escape. With a roar of triumph two of the men dropped armfuls of booty and lunged after her. There was a brief tussle, and then one of them, shrugging his shoulders, turned to argue with another soldier who was gathering up some of the things he had let fall, while the successful one dragged the screaming girl back into the house, urged on by the guffaws of his companions, and already tearing at her bodice as they disappeared.

Drusilla trembled, and then, with new anxiety, realised that a band of horsemen had ridden into the street. They were laying about them with the flats of their swords, and the soldiers quickly dispersed. The group halted under Drusilla's window, and she opened it a crack to listen to what they said.

"It is but a few wild, indisciplined men, my Lord Essex. I think it will cease now that we have shown we do not intend to condone it."

"That is what you said last time," Lord Essex replied. "However, all seems quiet now, and I do not propose to abandon my dinner altogether, so we will return to it again."

So saying, he turned and rode away, and Drusilla closed her eyes in momentary relief. She did not, however, share the belief that no more looting would take place, and was racking her brains for new methods of securing the house, and protecting the maids, when the door behind her opened.

She sprang up, seizing the knife, and faced the door, then gave a cry of relief and sped across the room to fling herself into Randal's arms.

Laughingly he removed the knife from her nerveless grasp, saying that he was relieved she had apparently still not learned to use a pistol, and between tears and laughter she gasped out that she thought he had left that morning.

"And leave you to that?" he asked, kissing her, so that she suddenly realised that she was clasped firmly in his arms, and was returning his embrace. In embarrassment she extricated herself, and stood shyly looking at him.

"You will not be able to protect the house from such as those men," he said gently. "Now will you come with me?"

She ignored the question.

"How did you get in? I thought all the doors were barred?"

"Yes, but I engaged Mistress Tanner's co-operation, for she agreed with me that you should leave the town. I have been waiting at her house, and when I saw how matters were I came through the gardens. Ned let me in.

"Mistress Tanner has been hiding you? But you are in danger!"

"No more than you. Now that you have seen the reality of men looting a defenceless town, despite promises of rewards if they did not, will you come with me?"

"But Meg and Joan! I could not leave them alone!"

"They will not be. Mistress Tanner will take them into her house, and her menservants and her sons will be sufficient protection. That rabble will seek easier prey."

" — Then I could go to her, too."

"To what purpose? That would not save James' property, and surely, now that you are alone, you wish to return to your parents? I can take you there now, with little risk, but who knows what might happen, and whether you would be able to travel to them during the summer, while the campaign is waged?"

"How could we leave?" Drusilla asked in a small voice, accepting his arguments, and firmly telling herself that it was the sense of them, not her desire to be with him, that made her agree.

"We'll go under cover of darkness, by boat, for they'll not have guards on the river. Mr Tanner says he can borrow one for us. When we came in by barge I left my horses at Sonning, and once there we can ride for Oxford or my home at Abingdon first, and then, if it is safe, to Devizes."

Thankfully Drusilla agreed, and Mistress Tanner almost cried with relief to learn that she had been persuaded. Joan, who had developed an admiration akin to worship for Mistress Drusilla since her rescue from the soldier, wept with dismay while Meg, her eyes round with wonder and her brain busy with speculation, thought that Mr Blagrave had had his nose put properly out of joint.

Mistress Tanner helped Drusilla select a few possessions to take with her in a bundle, and packed the rest, saying that she would send them on to Devizes as soon as the wagons were safe travelling that way again. She promised to tell James, should he appear, that Drusilla was safe, and Drusilla left a letter for her brother, expressing all her sorrow at Elizabeth's death, and hoping to see him again soon. When all was ready they locked up the house as securely as possible, and everyone, including the horses in the stables, left. Drusilla was sad to say farewell to her mare, but Randal comforted her by saying that no doubt she would soon be able to come for her, or have her sent to Devizes, and Willy, who was also to join the Tanners' household, promised to take the greatest care of her.

"They pesky rebels shan't get her, that I vow!"

Supper was as merry as it could be in a large family, overshadowed as it must be by Elizabeth's death, and when it was time to leave, Drusilla kissed her kind hostess warmly, promising that she would write as soon as she was able to tell of her safe arrival home.

"Thank you for all the help you have been to me," she said gratefully, and Mistress Tanner hugged her tightly.

"You'll be happy," she said obscurely.

"Best go the back way," one of her sons came in at that moment to say. "Mr Jacob Blagrave is knocking at your door, Mistress Matthews, and bawling to be let in as if a wolf were at his heels!"

Drusilla giggled, and with the escort of Mr Tanner and three of his sturdy sons, they crept out, trying to stifle their amusement.

The boat had been prepared earlier in the day, and was lying near a small wharf, concealed by a larger barge. Two of the Tanners were to accompany Drusilla and Sir Randal on the first stage of their journey, and bring the boat back, the same night or the next. The approach to the wharf was by a narrow lane, and they went in single file, keeping to the shadows. The lane was steep, and the ground rough, and they were half way along it when Mr Tanner's feet slipped on some loose pebbles and sent some of them clattering away, the noise seeming as loud as cannon fire in the silence of the night. They froze into immobility, and Sir Randal, who had been in front of Drusilla, turned and swiftly put his arm round her shoulders, giving her a comforting hug.

Dick Tanner, in the lead, drew out a knife from his belt as they heard footsteps to the front, and a voice demanding to know who was there. He was about to step forward when Sir Randal, pushing Drusilla back, spoke and moved into a patch of moonlight.

"It'sh me, ol' fellow," he muttered, contriving to scatter more of the loose stones underfoot. "I think I'm losht. Plaguey wench, her wine was bad! Wher'sh — confound it, I've forgot the name of shtreet! By a church! Aye, that'sh right, hard by a church!"

Mr Tanner stifled a chuckle as they listened to Sir Randal, mumbling somewhat incoherently, draw closer to the man who had spoken. Then another voice chimed in, and Drusilla gasped in dismay as she realised that there were two of them. Straining her eyes, she could distinguish vague shapes moving

131

in the shadows, and then, where the lane widened at the entrance to the wharf, she saw two men emerge from a doorway and into a greyer, dimly lit area.

Randal had moved quickly over the ground separating him from the two men, apparently unsteady with drink, and as he came up to them he grasped one by the arms, and began to explain at tedious length how he had been cheated and robbed and had now lost his way back to his billet. They were attempting to disengage from his persistence when, so suddenly that they did not even have time to cry out, he felled one man with a blow to the head and seized the other, twisting his arms behind him in a vicelike grip, and clamping one hand over his mouth to stifle any sounds.

The Tanners moved swiftly to help, and Dick was about to plunge his knife into the man Randal held when the latter prevented him.

"No, we have no need. Gag them and tie them, and we'll put them where they'll be found in the morning. Quietly now."

They did as he directed, and then, keeping an anxious watch for fear there were other soldiers about, set about the task of hauling in the boat from behind the barge, and settling into it. The Tanner brothers indignantly refused Sir Randal's offer to row, saying that he would be riding for most of the night, most likely, and they could rest when they wished, so he sat with Drusilla in the stern, and under cover of darkness took her hand in his and held it comfortingly.

Sonning was less than four miles downstream, and the farm where Sir Randal had left his horses was before the town, so they hoped to complete the journey in less than an hour. Moving cautiously through the town, they soon came into the open, and rowed past the ghostly tents in the river meadows. When they were safely past Dick Tanner whispered that there had been a vast amount of sickness in the camp.

"'Tis said they dug pits at Tilehurst to bury the dead, there were so many."

"Was that why they took so long to attack?" his brother Walter asked.

"Lord Essex appears a hesitant commander," Randal said. "He lost the initiative at Edge Hill, too, by failing to attack."

"Were you there, sir?"

"Oh, tell us what happened! It has all been rumour."

He was kept busy answering questions, and when they arrived at the small landing-stage which was their destination, the Tanners said that they could have wished for a row twice as long.

"You will find it harder returning upstream. Good fortune to you! Do not run risks, and pray give our thanks to your parents for all they have done. One day we will be able to thank you all properly."

"Thank you, indeed I am most grateful," Drusilla added, and stood with Sir Randal to wave until they had pulled out of sight.

"It is but a short distance. I trust my friends will not be too surprised to have me return at such an hour," Sir Randal said briskly, taking Drusilla's arm and guiding her along a path which led for a few yards along the river bank, and then turned to follow a hedge up a steep slope until they came to a cluster of farm buildings, faintly illuminated by the moonlight.

Quietly, Sir Randal led the way across a yard, halting when a dog barked. Then a window was flung open and a man called to know who was there.

"Sir Randal Thornton, Thomas," was the reply, and the window closed, a candle was lit, and Drusilla could see its faint glow as the farmer passed down the stairs and through an uncurtained room to open the kitchen door.

"Welcome, sir. I heard that you'd left Reading, and was expecting you earlier, but the others said you had been delayed. Nought serious, I trust?"

"It depends on your viewpoint," Randal replied with a laugh. "I had to escort the lady. We must leave at once, Thomas, and put as many miles as possible between ourselves and the Roundheads before daylight. Can you ride a man's saddle, Drusilla?"

"Yes, I often did as a child," she answered, and the farmer regarded her with approval.

"If you'd not think it an impertinence, Mistress, I could find you an old pair of breeches, which would be more comfortable, and also help to hide the fact that you're a woman riding so."

"The very thing!" Drusilla exclaimed, and the gratified farmer bustled off to procure a pair of somewhat tattered, but clean and suitable breeches.

Shown into a small room off the kitchen, Drusilla had soon divested herself of her petticoats and stuffed them into her bundle. The breeches were a few sizes too large for her slim form, but she discovered some twine in one of the pockets and tied it about her waist, then returned to the kitchen, suddenly blushing as she saw the admiration in both men's eyes.

"Here is some ale and bread and cheese," Thomas said hurriedly, and thankfully she sat down and tried to forget her unconventional attire.

They were soon riding away, Drusilla on a small compact mare that had no difficulty in keeping pace with Randal's own horse. The moon had risen, and they were able to make good speed, covering most of the distance towards Oxford before the dawn.

"Are you tired?" Randal asked, as they

paused to eat some more bread and cheese Thomas had provided.

"A little. How far is it now?" Drusilla asked, lying back on the cloak he had spread out for them.

"That village to the left is Dorchester. It is about ten miles, slightly less, to Oxford. But my own home is less than five miles away, towards Abingdon, and since Oxford is like to be unpleasantly crowded, I suggest I take you to Thornton Hall and leave you in the care of my sister, who is living there for the moment, while I go into Oxford and discover what I can of the situation, whether it is safe to set out for Devizes after you have had an opportunity to rest."

"Your sister?" Drusilla queried anxiously.

"Jane is some years older than I, with a daughter of fifteen. Her husband died a year since, and she is living with me until she marries again, which she plans to do this summer. She will make you very welcome, there is no cause to fear her."

Drusilla smiled tremulously.

"I think I would prefer that to Oxford, especially in these clothes," she said breathlessly, and Randal suppressed the desire to take her in his arms and tell her just how delectable she was, despite being tired and dirty and attired in ragged breeches much too large for her. Instead, he rose to his feet and attended to the horses.

"You look charmingly," he said in a neutral tone, "but mayhap not conventional enough for the Court! Come, we will soon be there, and you will be able to sleep for as long as you wish!"

He lifted her up into the saddle, and they set off again. Drusilla was almost dropping with weariness when they rode into a large stableyard, and she took very little notice of the house or its surroundings, beyond a dim realisation that it was a mellow stone house, perhaps a hundred years old, covered with creeping plants, many of which were beginning to flower and clothe the house in their bright colours.

Randal had to lift her from the saddle, as a startled stableboy came running out of one of the many doorways to take the horses, but she straightened her shoulders and assured him that although she was exceedingly stiff she could walk into the house. She retained a confused impression of a large, somewhat overpowering lady exclaiming in amazement, and then she was led to a pleasantly furnished room by a motherly housekeeper, who bade her not to talk, and ruthlessly stripped off her clothes before tucking her into what Drusilla, on the verge of sleep, thought must be the most comfortable bed in the world.

She awoke at dusk, and a maid sitting beside her told her that Sir Randal had given orders that she was not to make any attempt to get up, but was to eat and then go back to sleep again. Drusilla chuckled but was only too ready, once her hunger had been satisfied with some delicious veal pie and an omelette flavoured with herbs, accompanied by an excellent glass of wine, to obey the instructions.

The sun was shining through the windows when next she awoke, and she found that one of the gowns she had brought with her, a rose coloured one trimmed with blonde lace, had been unpacked from her bundle and the creases ironed out. She got out of bed, rubbing her still aching limbs ruefully, and dressed, tying back her curls with a matching ribbon. Tentatively, she opened the door of the room and found that it led into a wide gallery, at the end of which were some shallow, curving stairs that led down into the great hall, furnished with massive oak tables and chairs, and with a faded but still lovely tapestry hanging on the wall opposite the enormous fireplace.

A large dog rose to his feet as she appeared on the stairs, and moved ponderously towards her, his tail waving in welcome. Drusilla, after her expeditions on the downs with her shepherd friend, when she had watched him handling many wild animals, had no fear of dogs, and came unhesitatingly down the stairs, holding out her hand for the dog to sniff.

"You are a beauty, are you not?" she said, patting him on the head, and then turned suddenly as a laugh came from a doorway on her left.

A girl some years younger than herself, but most fashionably dressed, stood there, looking at her in candid admiration.

"Are you not afraid?" she asked.

Drusilla laughed.

"Should I be? He looks to be friendly enough."

"Oh, yes, Uncle Randal says that Nero would not hurt a kitten, but Mary screamed when she first saw him, and still will not be alone with him."

"Mary?" Drusilla said, her heart suddenly cold.

"Mary Percy. Mama says that Uncle Randal is going to marry her, though I wish that he would choose someone less — less beautiful!" the girl said.

"Oh, is she beautiful?" Drusilla asked, her heart sinking even lower.

"Vastly, and it is so depressing to feel that people are for ever comparing us! She has big blue eyes, and truly golden hair, not just fair like mine, and a pink and white complexion. She is small, but has a most shapely figure. All the Court are mad for her, and Mama says that Uncle Randal is fortunate to have captured her, for besides all that, she has a simply enormous fortune, and important relatives who will be of great use to Uncle Randal when this wretched war is over, and he can be a courtier again instead of a soldier. She makes me feel so big and clumsy. Why should some girls have everything, when I am not even pretty, and have a mere pittance, besides a tendency to freckles!"

"And a tongue which is a deal too busy," another voice chimed in, and the large lady Drusilla recalled from the previous morning came out of the room, holding her hands out to Drusilla and smiling down at her. "You poor child," she went on, drawing Drusilla into the room. "Randal has said how you have suffered, and we all intend to look after you until you can be restored to your parents. Now come and break your fast."

Trying to talk sensibly when all she could think of was the lovely, rich, aristocratic and influential Mary Percy, Drusilla did not dare to ask where Randal was, but his niece, who was introduced to her as Barbara, soon informed her that he had ridden off to Oxford the previous day.

"He went after dinner, saying that he had rested enough, and had much to do," she explained, and Drusilla wondered if he had been anxious to return to Mary. She started when she found her thoughts echoed by Mistress Jane Burton.

"No doubt he wished to pay his respects to Mistress Percy before asking audience of the King," she said, smiling at Drusilla. "It is fortunate that Randal has returned, for Mistress Percy is coming to visit me, and he can escort her here tomorrow. I hope that she will be company for you while we are making arrangements to send you home," she added. "A charming girl, and considering her advantages, so very unassuming."

Drusilla muttered something suitable, but it did not appear to matter that she could make so inadequate a reply. Mistress Burton, like her daughter, had a busy tongue, and did not seem to desire answers to her observations.

"Thornton Hall is so lovely in the spring," she went on. "I did so want Mary to see it at this time of year, and it is fortunate that I can be here to play hostess, for as you may know, I am about to marry again myself, and soon Mary — well, you heard my chatterbox of a daughter, and it is no great secret — we expect that she will soon wed my brother."

Somehow Drusilla endured the meal, and afterwards, pleading that she was still tired from her journey and the strain of nursing her sister-in-law, apart from the anxiety of the siege, evaded Barbara's offer to show her round the house and escaped to her room. There she dissolved into helpless tears, weeping both for the loss of the gentle Elizabeth, whom she had grown to love dearly, and even more for the crumbling of the hopes she had rashly permitted to rise again during the past two days.

6

IT was half way through the afternoon on the following day, and Barbara had been showing Drusilla the knot garden, when the sounds of arrivals came from the nearby stable yard.

"It must be Uncle Randal and Mistress Percy," Barbara said in great excitement, and picking up her skirts she ran to the doorway which led through the walled kitchen garden and then to the stables. Reluctantly Drusilla followed her, to find Randal in the process of lifting down from her saddle the loveliest creature Drusilla had ever seen. Ethereally fair, with a delicately moulded face and figure, Mistress Percy was incomparable, and it was no wonder, Drusilla thought miserably, that Randal lingered as he set her on her feet, and she coquettishly looked up into his eyes and murmured something.

The visitor then turned with an enchanting smile to greet her hostess, who had just appeared, and Randal strode across to where Drusilla waited a few feet away. He took her hands in his, and then looked searchingly at her.

"My dear, you are pale! Are you well?"

"I am perfectly well, I thank you, but still somewhat weary," Drusilla replied in a low voice, and there was no time for more as Mistress Burton was calling to Drusilla, saying that she wished to present her to Mistress Percy.

Mary greeted her prettily, but shot a quick glance from her to Randal, then gently chided him for having forced Mistress Matthews to ride so far.

"It was brutal of you, Randal! Poor creature, she still looks exhausted from it! I do not know how you could have endured it!" she went on, turning back to Drusilla.

"It was not only the ride," Drusilla said calmly. "I am accustomed to long hours in the saddle, and it was urgent to get as far away from Reading as we could."

"Indeed, yes! How did you survive the siege? You must tell me all about it. I long to hear. I know that I should die if I were in such a predicament!"

146

"You would astonish us all, and yourself, no doubt, by being as valiant as Drusilla," Randal said with a smile at her, and was then somewhat coldly recalled to his duties as host when Mistress Burton asked whether they intended to remain in the stables all day. He offered Mary his arm, and turned to offer the other to Drusilla, to find his sister already ushering her into the house.

Mistress Burton informed Randal that she had left his steward in the small winter parlour, anxiously waiting to discuss several urgent matters since he had been away for several weeks. Having then quellingly asked Barbara and Drusilla whether they could entertain themselves for a while, she escorted Mary Percy to her room. It was suppertime before they met again, and then Randal was able to give them news from Oxford.

"The Queen is still in York but plans to rejoin the King soon. Oxford is being fortified, and the meadows of Christchurch have been flooded in aid of this."

"Poor meadows!" Mary commented. "They are so lovely in the spring,

Mistress Matthews. Mayhap, when this war is over, you will be able to come from Devizes to visit them."

"We heard that Hopton had been routed in the west," Mistress Burton said. "Is it true?"

"A minor setback, and the Parliamentarians make too much of it, by all accounts. As they do of Waller's small victory in the Marches."

"Waller?" Drusilla interjected, and Randal smiled at her understandingly.

"There have been a few minor engagements, but nothing of any moment," he said reassuringly.

"Did you not say that your brother was serving under Waller?" Barbara asked, and Mary looked at Drusilla in horror.

"He is a rebel?" she breathed incredulously.

"Many families are divided, as you know well," Randal intervened quickly, preventing Drusilla from replying, and then he went on to tell of the reports they had received from London of the poor conditions there, the many beggars, the disruption of trading and the general discontent. "If all this is true, the war may soon be over."

"Oh, how I pray for that!" Mary exclaimed, turning to smile at Randal. "Then we can all return to normal life, can we not?"

"Some might find it dull afterwards," he said teasingly, and Drusilla looked away, unable to watch with adequate composure the pair of them and the terms of intimacy they were on.

After more talk of the war, Mistress Burton asked Randal what arrangements he intended to make for Drusilla.

"It is not that I wish you to leave us, my dear," she said to Drusilla, "but that I fear your parents, learning of the capture of Reading, must be exceedingly anxious about you, and you doubtless wish to reassure them of your safety at the earliest possible moment."

"Drusilla is hardly fit to set out immediately," Randal said firmly. "Besides, I have to wait a day or so for instructions. I have persuaded the King to send me to Cornwall on a mission so that I can combine duty with pleasure and escort Drusilla as I promised her."

"You mean to leave again almost at

149

once?" Mary said with a provocative pout of the lips. "Oh, that is too bad!"

"Will it not delay you to have to go to Devizes?" his sister asked, frowning. "I am certain that we could provide Mistress Matthews with a strong escort, and then she would be able to remain here for as long as necessary, until she is fully recovered."

"I think another two days will be sufficient, and Devizes is directly on my way. Besides, I promised Drusilla to see her safely home."

"Well, let us hope your mission in Cornwall will not take you away from us for too long, brother. In the meantime, Mary, I will be able to show you all over the house," she added significantly.

Drusilla had no opportunity of private speech with Randal, and she was not certain that she wanted it. It was clear from his sister's behaviour that she regarded Mary as already betrothed to him, and Mary behaved with a sweetly possessive air that Randal appeared to enjoy. She had been a fool to read anything more than a casual friendliness or sympathy in a few easily given kisses,

Drusilla told herself fiercely as she prepared for bed that night. No doubt he was wishing her at the devil, and no doubt also that if this mission to Sir Ralph Hopton in Cornwall had not been given him, he would have been ready enough to accept his sister's suggestion of sending someone else to escort Drusilla to Devizes. It was only his good manners, she thought, that made him refuse to show how tedious he must regard the burden she was to him.

On the following day, a group of horsemen appeared riding up the long avenue which led to the house, and reined in before the massive front door. Drusilla, to escape having to listen to Mary telling Randal news of all their friends in Oxford, had slipped out of the house and was slowly returning from a walk across the meadows that separated it from a thick belt of trees some hundred yards away, so was unable to avoid the visitors. She halted, eyeing them doubtfully as they dismounted, talking gaily, but was forced to approach when Randal appeared on the steps and, seeing her hesitating a short distance away, hailed her.

"Welcome, Your Highnesses," he was saying as she reached the group, and then she found the renowned Prince Rupert, tall, debonair and dashingly handsome, bowing over her hand.

"I am charmed to meet you, Mistress Matthews. Randal has been singing your praises so loudly that I had to come and see you for myself. I understand you disarmed a ruffian who was attacking him, and for that alone, saving him for us, you have my most grateful thanks!"

The Prince's brother, Maurice, a younger and in every way slightly smaller version of him, was then introduced, and the other men, all young and merry, but Drusilla was so overwhelmed that she could not afterwards recall a single name or face apart from those of the Princes.

"We are come to dinner, as you suggested," Prince Rupert announced, as they strolled along the terrace before the house. "I have your instructions, and you are to set out tomorrow. Be sure to hasten back to us, Randal, for I have many plans for harrassing the rebels, and your knowledge of this area will be of tremendous assistance. We can descend on London itself, if we've a mind to it, from our garrisons at Abingdon and Wallingford. That would frighten the good citizens, no?"

After three hours of his energetic company, Drusilla felt that she knew now why he had the reputation he did, for courage and leadership in his famous cavalry charges, and enterprise in outwitting the enemy, but she thought that his very energy and impatience would set more cautious people against him. When he and his friends eventually left, Randal turned to Drusilla.

"I am pleased to see that you look more restored today. Will you be able to ride tomorrow? We should be able to do the journey in one day if we start early and rest on the way."

"Yes, I am quite able to ride so far," Drusilla said, but with a sinking heart, for in all probability it would be the last day she would spend with him, the last time she would ever see him, and soon he would be wed to the lovely Mary Percy.

Early on the following morning, they rode away from Thornton Hall, and although she expressed regret at losing her unexpected visitor so soon, Mistress Burton did not give the impression of being sorry to see the last of her. Of the two ladies, Mary Percy seemed to have a more genuine regret at parting, but Drusilla cynically told herself that this could only be because Mary was perturbed at the thought of Randal being alone in Drusilla's company all day.

They left Abingdon and Wantage behind them, and then crossed Lambourne Downs. Until they rode up on to the downs, they had been passing through many tiny villages, and the roads had been busy. They met a couple of foraging parties from the Abingdon garrison, and there were many wagons and pack ponies carrying goods to sell to the King's army. On the downs, however, it was quiet and peaceful, and Drusilla was surprised when she looked back to see three more travellers taking the same track.

"We have company," she said to Randal, indicating them, and he looked back, frowning.

"Aye, and there is something about them I do not like. I am certain that I saw one of them passing the main gates as we left the Hall."

"You think they are following us? Who could it be?" Drusilla asked in alarm.

"Oh, no doubt I am wrong, unduly suspicious. But Drusilla, I want you to promise that if aught should happen to me, you will gallop away as fast as you can! I still have not taught you to use a pistol!" he added with a laugh.

"I could not leave you!" she protested.

"You must be sensible," he said firmly, and as she appeared about to argue, went on persuasively, "If you stay, we are both in more danger, since they will want to dispose of witnesses. If you can escape, you could possibly obtain help from the nearest house or village."

Reluctantly, as he insisted, Drusilla promised to do her utmost to escape, and she kept looking back over her shoulder apprehensively, her anxieties lessening slightly when she saw that the riders, whoever they were, made no attempt to narrow the distance between them.

"We will halt for a rest and some food in Lambourne," Randal said, as they came in sight of the town, and they found an inn overlooking the river where they procured a roasted chicken, some rabbit pie, and some excellent ale.

Randal had been watching from the window and saw the other travellers go past. They did not appear to have noticed that Randal and Drusilla had halted, and did not give the inn a second glance, being apparently much more interested in watching some village girls who were beside the river. After a lengthy rest Randal suggested that it was time for them to be on their way again, and called for the horses.

Two miles further on, they were passing through a small copse when the report of a pistol sounded close to them. Drusilla's horse reared in fright and she had considerable difficulty in preventing the terrified animal from bolting. By the time she had brought him under control again she realised that Randal was struggling to fight off two men who had closed in on either side, while another, still in the shadows cast by the trees, was levelling a pistol at him, but was apparently unable to fire because of the mêlée of figures in the roadway.

Completely forgetting her promise,

Drusilla urged her reluctant mount closer to the fray, and raising her whip brought it down sharply on the head of the man nearest her. He turned with an oath, and Randal, who had drawn his sword, was able to render him of no further threat by a timely thrust at his shoulder. The other attacker tried to close in while Randal's attention was so engaged, but with a rapid movement Randal twisted his sword and brought it swinging round and down towards the other. He attempted to move sideways, but the sword glanced off his shoulder, tearing the stuff of his doublet, and the point then made a jagged cut in his thigh, which was soon spouting crimson blood. The man under the trees fired wildly as Randal turned towards him, though still keeping well under cover. The shot missed Randal, but the bullet lacerated Drusilla's arm in the upper, fleshy part, and the searing pain caused her to gasp and, as she clutched at her injured arm, let go the reins so that the terrified horse, having no restraint on him, threw her to the ground as he made for the trees.

The armed man had turned and gone,

followed by his wounded companions. Randal leapt down from his horse and ran to where Drusilla lay motionless. A swift examination showed that the bullet had scratched a deep cut on her arm, and this was bleeding freely, but it was the fall which had knocked her senseless. As he lifted her in his arms, she groaned and her eyelids flickered, then she lay still, scarcely breathing.

Randal's own mount, not unaccustomed to the sound of firing pistols or being involved in hand to hand struggles, had remained where Randal had left him, and begun to nibble the grass at the side of the road. Randal carried Drusilla and carefully lifted her on to the saddle before him, contriving to mount without shaking her too much. He recalled seeing a small inn some few hundred yards back along the road, and judged it the closest place for seeking help, so he turned his horse and guided it gently back until this small building was reached.

There were two women standing gossiping by the door and they exclaimed in horror when Randal rode up to them, for apart from still lying supine in Randal's arms, Drusilla's gown was muddy and bloodstained.

"Pray fetch mine host," Randal ordered, and one of the women darted into the inn while the other came across to help him hold Drusilla steady while he carefully dismounted.

"A bed, at once!" he said, lifting her down and carrying her into the inn, where a flustered innkeeper met him, and while talking volubly about the wicked soldiers who were ravaging the countryside, led the way up some steep narrow stairs to fling open one of the two small doors at the top and indicate to Randal that he was to enter.

Randal had to bend his head to pass under the low doorway, and he found the room to be small and roughly furnished with a small bed and a table, with a rickety chair beside the window. Laying Drusilla down upon the bed, Randal turned to the innkeeper who hovered by the door, seeming unwilling to enter.

"Send someone to fetch the nearest surgeon, if you please, and bring me water and clean linen immediately."

The man nodded.

"There's a doctor in Lambourne, if he be there at this time," he said eagerly. "If not, I do believe there be one at Wantage."

"Make sure that whoever you send does not come back without one or the other, or I'll make him wish he'd not come back at all!" was the only response he received, and he hastened to obey this imperious guest.

As the innkeeper bowed himself out of the room, the woman who had helped Randal lift Drusilla down appeared, carrying a bowl of warm water and some clean rags.

"Shall I be attending to her cuts?" she asked, and Randal smiled briefly at her.

"It is no cut, Mistress, but a pistol graze. Not serious, I warrant, but it has bled profusely."

"Then I've a salve that would be just the thing to soothe it," she offered. "I'll fetch it at once."

She went off, and Randal took his dagger and slit the sleeve of Drusilla's gown to lay bare the wound. To his relief it did not seem any worse than he had first thought, and by the time he had washed it the woman was back and was offering him a small pot full of a sweet-smelling unguent. He thanked her briefly and covered the wound with it, then bound Drusilla's arm tightly.

"Did she swoon?" the woman asked, looking at Drusilla's still lifeless form.

"No, her horse was startled and threw her," he replied. "I think there is a bruise on her head, but I did not wait to examine her closely."

As he spoke, he was gently easing Drusilla's curls aside, and revealed a swelling on the side of her head.

"Oh, 'tis bad, sir! How long ago?"

"A few minutes only. Did you not hear the firing? The villains shot at us twice."

The woman shook her head.

"It was too far away, no doubt, and the trees deaden sound. Do you know who they were? Did they seek to rob you, or were they soldiers?"

"I do not think they were robbers or soldiers," he said slowly. "Have you been troubled much by either?"

She shrugged.

"Those foolish enough to leave their

sheep or cattle untended these days find them gone. And now, I hear tell, we are asked for heavy taxes to pay for the war! It seems daft to me! Why cannot folk be sensible and agree?"

At that moment, Drusilla stirred slightly, and Randal, who had seated himself beside her on the bed, took her hand gently in his.

"Drusilla," he said softly, and her eyelids fluttered, and she sighed.

"She will be sensible soon," the woman predicted. "I'll take away the water and rags."

She did so, and within a few minutes Drusilla opened her eyes and looked up at Randal.

"Hush, my love, don't talk, you are safe!" he said, and she smiled up at him, then winced as she felt the swelling on her head.

"My head hurts!" she whispered. "What happened?"

"You were thrown when the horse bolted, startled by the shots."

"Shots? My head? And my arm, too?"

"The bullet grazed your arm, that is all. The lump on your head is where you fell, and now you must not talk any more."

"Where are we?" she asked, ignoring his command.

"At a small inn nearby. I have sent for a surgeon, and you must lie still until he sees you. Try to rest."

"Are you hurt? I remember now, some men. Who were they?"

"I did not see," he replied. "You came to my aid again, my dear, when I had expressly forbidden you to intervene. Mayhap they would have dispatched me if you had not, so again I owe you my life. But I had rather you had not been hurt, my sweetest love!"

She smiled again, and with a sigh drifted back into a half-conscious state. Randal watched her anxiously, and was heartily relieved when the woman who had helped him so competently previously, and who had proved to be the innkeeper's wife, knocked softly on the door and announced that the surgeon had arrived.

He was an elderly man, but he appeared to know what he was about, and after a swift examination of Drusilla's head, turned to Randal.

"I will not disturb the bandage to see

the other wound, for if Mistress Saddler assisted you I can be satisfied until tomorrow, for she is a skilled nurse. I do not like the head wound, though, the humours appear to be badly affected. I will bleed the young lady, and come again tomorrow.

He was laying out his instruments as he talked, and with a nod and a smile, turned back to take Drusilla's uninjured arm and swiftly open a vein and withdraw some blood. She stirred slightly, and once opened her eyes during the process, but relapsed into insensibility almost immediately. There was nothing else to be done apart from keep a close watch on her, he said, as he rose to depart, promising again to be there on the following day.

Towards late afternoon, Drusilla roused enough to ask Randal where they were. She appeared to have forgotten about the attack, and he answered her briefly, saying that she had been hurt and must rest. He attempted to give her some broth Mistress Saddler had prepared, but after a mouthful she pushed it away, and again slipped into unconsciousness.

Deeply concerned at these prolonged effects of her fall, Randal remained watching over her, setting a candle where its glow could not disturb her when darkness came. As the night wore on, Drusilla became restless, and tossed on the bed, apparently oblivious to the pain of her wounds, for she made no attempt to avoid turning on to them. Her skin was dry and feverish, and Randal, anxious to keep the bedcoverings over her, for the night was chill, and the room boasted no fireplace, found that she could be quietened when he held her cradled in his arms, and he could keep her well covered and also protect her wounded arm and head, preventing her from injuring them further.

As he sat on the bed with her cradled in his arms, the candle finally gutted, and he realised that the dawn would soon appear. Drusilla had been quieter for the past hour, and her fever seemed to have lessened, and some time after the first birds had heralded a new day, she stirred, opening her eyes and looking up into his.

"Oh, my head!" she exclaimed, as she

moved slightly. Then she frowned, and tried to look about her. "What in the world has happened? Where are we? What is amiss?"

"You have been feverish, and the only way to prevent you from throwing off all the covers, or rolling over on to your arm, was to imprison you!" he replied lightly, and laid her back on to the pillows, sliding off the bed and standing looking down at her with an expression in his eyes that caused Drusilla to bite her lip and drop her own gaze.

"You have sat with me all night? Oh, Randal, I am sorry! You must be exceedingly tired!"

"It has served its purpose, however, and you seem vastly improved. Are you hungry?"

She laughed.

"I had not thought of it, but yes, I am! But pray tell me what happened! I can recall a fight, and my horse bolted! I thought I was a better horsewoman than to permit that!"

"We were attacked, and you were shot in the arm," he replied briefly. "It was just a graze, but your horse did not appreciate the explosion, and while you were distracted, he threw you. That caused the wound on your head which has kept you in pain. Now I will arrange for some breakfast, and you must rest until the doctor comes to see you later today."

Drusilla, feeling weaker than ever before, smiled gratefully, and Randal went out to fetch Mistress Saddler. She had some food taken up to Drusilla by a young girl who was helping her in the kitchen, and after telling Randal to help himself to what was set out on the kitchen table, commented that he would be wise to take a sleep himself after he had eaten. She then went upstairs to see whether Drusilla needed any help.

When she returned, she reported that in her opinion Drusilla was recovering fast, but would need to stay in bed for some time.

"There's a bed for you, sir, in the other room, and I'll rouse you when the doctor comes. I'll sit with your — the young lady, you can leave her safely to my care."

"Indeed, I can," Randal said gratefully. "We were most fortunate to find such help."

He looked in on Drusilla again, but she was sleeping, peacefully this time, and Mistress Saddler was sitting beside her bed, so he was content to seek his own for a couple of hours before the doctor arrived.

The doctor expressed himself satisfied with the progress of the bullet wound and the bruises to the head, but told Drusilla that she was not to stir out of her bed for at least two days.

"Then I'll see you again, my dear, and say whether you and your husband can continue your journey."

Fortunately for Drusilla he had turned to Randal as he spoke, and missed her sudden flush. She glanced apprehensively at Randal, and blushed even more to see that he was regarding her with a curious smile on his lips. Had he really spoken words of love to her, or was it a dream born of her own longing recalled from her earlier delirious state? She had no way of telling, and tried to dismiss the recollection, not daring to hope that it might be true.

"I have recalled that you were on a mission to Cornwall," she said hurriedly when he returned after seeing the doctor off. "It has delayed you already, I fear, and I must not be the cause of more delay. I am perfectly safe here, and I think you should leave me."

"My mission can wait," he replied with a laugh. "Are you ashamed of the good doctor's assumption? I fear Mistress Saddler is puzzled, too, for she has been in some doubt as to how to refer to you!"

"Oh, dear, it is so difficult for you!" Drusilla said in a small voice. "But you must go! I can ride home when I am better — that is, if you will ask the innkeeper to arrange for a horse, since I suppose the brute that threw me is lost?"

"And have you attacked by such villains again?" he asked lightly. "No, indeed!"

"I wonder who they were? Did you discover aught about them?" she asked, diverted for a moment.

"The one who shot you was very concerned not to be seen," he told her. "I suspect therefore that he was known to me. The others, poor fools as they were, must have been hirelings whose identity did not matter."

"But that need not happen — my being attacked again," she went on. "I have been thinking, and if a message were to be sent to my father, he could come himself, or send one of his own men, to escort me home."

"No. I promised to see you safely there, and although I have not been very efficient as yet, I intend to complete the task, my dear!"

Seeing that he could not be moved, Drusilla again began to speculate on who the attackers could have been, but Randal did not seem to be very interested, saying that it was most likely some supporter of Parliament who had recognised him as one of the King's men, and had determined to wage a little private campaign. Then, seeing that she was inclined to worry about it, he talked of other things, mainly describing the Court and the people there, until she fell asleep.

Drusilla gradually recovered her strength, and on the third day the doctor permitted her to rise from her bed. He warned her, however, that it would be several days

170

before she felt well enough to ride, and so it proved. It was a week after the attack before she was able to resume the journey, and then they set off, bidding a grateful farewell to the friendly Saddlers.

7

DRUSILLA was still very weak, and Randal insisted on breaking the journey at Marlborough. She protested, feeling guilty all the time at the delay to his mission, but he insisted that it was not urgent, and the only one who would be concerned at the time he was taking was Prince Rupert.

"And that only for the help I can give him in harassing the enemy," he said laughingly. "In fact, he is perfectly capable of doing all he wishes without my help!"

"There is also Mistress Percy, who will be expecting you back!" Drusilla said in a low voice.

"Mary will be perfectly content with Jane, examining the house, and the two of them will delight in reorganising it for me! While Rupert is harassing Lord Essex, my housekeeper and the gardener and the cook will all be equally harassed by the two of them making suggestions!

Are all women the same? Did you not wish to alter the way things were done, my dear?"

"It was not my place to even think of it!" Drusilla said indignantly, and then, since this sounded as though she was being critical of Mary Percy and his sister, hurriedly added that she had no experience of great houses, merely modest town ones, and did not know how things should be done, in any event.

"It is not so very different, I think. I do not live in great pomp, as some of Mary's relatives do, for instance. My parents both died before I was twenty, and I have missed the family life they provided. Jane is an excellent sister, but has her own family, and cares too much for position and pride of rank, rather than happiness. She will be well satisfied with her new husband, and though I should not, I cannot help but be relieved that his main estate is in Yorkshire! She will not be able to visit me very often! I would like to see more of Barbara, though. Did you like her?"

"I thought she was very pleasant," Drusilla said slowly, and became so lost in her own thoughts that Randal had to speak twice before she heard his next remark.

"You are tired," he said, looking at her in concern. "We shall be in Marlborough in less than half an hour, and you will not argue!" he forestalled her protests. "I am determined on staying!"

She really was finding the journey exhausting, and was glad to submit. After dinner and a rest, however, she was restored enough to walk slowly through the town with him, and sit for a while beside the river. Because of her exertions and the day in the open, she slept long that night, and it was consequently rather advanced in the morning when they set out on the last part of their journey to Devizes.

It was a beautiful spring day, and Drusilla was feeling almost her old self, apart from the oppression caused to her spirits by the thought that this was, at last, her final day with Randal. However, she tried to disguise her mood and pointed out the landmarks as they drew near to Devizes. They rode across the rolling downs, and Randal, unlike

Drusilla, seemed to be in high spirits that made him increasingly light-hearted the further they went.

It was because he was at last to be rid of her, Drusilla told herself miserably, and became silent for a while. Then she roused herself as they breasted one hill, and pointing with her whip told him that Devizes lay in the valley beyond the next rise.

"That is Roundway Hill before us," she explained. "The ground falls steeply beyond it towards the town. It is the edge of the downs, for to our right there is a much steeper hill dropping to the plain. My father's home is in the Market Place."

They rode across the wide expanse of Roundway Hill, and down the further, steeper side, into Roundway village, in silence. Then, as they approached the town, Drusilla asked, in a strained voice, whether Randal proposed to ride further that day.

"My parents will be so grateful to you for all you have done for me," she said shyly, "and they will wish to offer you hospitality. But I have delayed you for so long, and again today since you would not have me woken early! You may wish to leave at once."

"You sound as though you wished to be rid of me!" he said teasingly, and she turned her head away from him to hide the tear trembling on her lashes.

"Not at all, but you must not feel any more obligation towards me," she stammered.

"Indeed? I feel no obligation, my dear, but I have a wish to see Devizes. However, since it might incommode your parents to have us both unexpectedly appear, I will take a room at an inn. Which is the best one?"

"The Crown, in St John's Street," she replied, "but if you wish to remain, I know that my mother would be proud to have you stay in her house."

"Proud?" he queried, with a smile and raised eyebrows. "I hope she will welcome me, but nonetheless I will suggest the inn, for I do not wish to impose."

They fell silent again and Drusilla led the way while Randal gazed about him at the little town. Their arrival was observed by a young girl who had been walking through the wide Market Place, idly swinging a basket, but when she saw Drusilla she gaped, and then ran across to a large, prosperous looking house, and shouted something as she ran inside.

They halted outside the house, and Randal had just lifted Drusilla down from her saddle when a middle-aged woman, followed by the girl, came to the door, exclaiming as she swept forward, her arms outstretched, and clasped Drusilla to her ample bosom.

"My love, my dearest, how have you come?" she asked, kissing Drusilla and hugging her. "We thought — oh, all manner of things — when we heard that you had disappeared. But come in, come in, and — who is the gentleman?"

She turned, puzzled, to Randal, and Drusilla hastened to present him.

"Sir Randal Thornton, my mother!"

They eventually, between exclamations and laughter, got themselves inside, and the maid Betty fetched wine to the parlour, while Drusilla tried to answer all her mother's questions, and Randal interposed to add his own explanations when it seemed necessary.

"Sir Randal, we owe you such a great deal for taking such good care of our dear Drusilla. You will stay for dinner? My husband will be here soon. Oh, I am so distracted!"

Fortunately, Mr Matthews, told the news of his daughter's sudden arrival with a strange young man by the excited maid, appeared at that moment in the parlour, and after he had also heard the main story, Mistress Matthews declared that she must ensure that the maids were not too excited to be preparing dinner, and bore Drusilla off with her.

Randal refused all the urgings of Drusilla's parents, and insisted that since he must make an early start on the following day he would spent the night at the Crown. He went off immediately dinner was finished, promising to return when he had bestowed his belongings. Mr Matthews smiled approvingly at Drusilla when he had left.

"Well, daughter, you have been cleverer than I could have expected!"

Drusilla looked puzzled.

"Oh, yes, I thought that you had too many romantic notions when you refused all those suitable offers. I had no inkling that you had your sights on higher game!"

"I don't understand!"

"Keep that innocent look, my dear, it will serve you well! Yes, Sir Randal Thornton is an excellent match, richer than I could have hoped for, and a title to boot!"

"Sir Randal? A match!"

"He feels just as he ought, my dear, and after the past few days, alone in your company, travelling and staying openly at inns, what else could he do? He has behaved excellently, and I congratulate you, I do indeed. I do not think you will regret it. It was very astute of you to play on that bump to the head, my dear. A pity in some ways that you are not a man, for you'd do excellently in business. However, I shall be very proud of my daughter, Lady Thornton!"

Drusilla was looking horrified.

"Me? Lady Thornton? I do not understand! You are mistaken!"

"Oh, come, you need not pretend with me! A merchant's daughter has just as much honour as the daughter of a lord!

Their reputations must be protected also, and having compromised you Sir Randal could do nought else than offer to wed you. He would be ruined if he did not, I can tell you, for although I do not have a title, I do have some influence! But I do not fear there will be trouble, for he seems an honourable man."

"Father, what are you saying? That Sir Randal has offered marriage because we were forced to stay alone at public inns?"

Her father laughed.

"Surely that was your plan when you pleaded a head wound?"

"But I was injured!" she protested. "It was no such plan as you suggest! I would not!"

"Oh, come, I do not say that you planned it all, down to the bullet wound, which your mother assures me is the merest scratch, for how could you? But you did very cleverly use the tumble from your horse!"

"I was ill — for days!" Drusilla insisted, but he would not be convinced, saying that a knock on the head was nothing, and she had been clever to fool the doctor, too.

"No, I cannot permit it! It would be wrong, for he wishes to wed Mary Percy!"

"Oho? So you have contrived to snatch him from another girl? Either I did not know you well before you went away, my dear, or you learned a great deal in Reading!"

Drusilla protested and explained in vain; her father refused to believe that she had not intended to trap Sir Randal into making an offer of marriage, and eventually Drusilla sought her own room to ponder this problem in peace. What must Randal think of her? She pushed aside the temptation to permit matters to take their course. He did not love her, for in her semi-conscious state she must have dreamed those few words of love. If not, why had he not hinted at his feelings when she had recovered her senses? She was convinced that Randal, having realised the unfortunate dilemma they found themselves in, had indeed agreed to marry her to protect her reputation, despite his love for Mary, and although she was sure that she could make him happier than Mary could if he loved her, the fact that he had been forced to marry her would always have come between them, and he would hate her, and resent her for being the cause of his loss. She could not bear the thought, or wish to deprive him of the girl he really wanted, for she loved him too deeply.

Eventually, Drusilla determined that whatever her father said or did, she would steadfastly refuse to accept Sir Randal, and he would have to depart. She did not think he would be willing to take part in a marriage if he knew that it was being forced on her, whatever the scandal threatened by her father, and so there was little risk that she would be compelled. As she was well aware, parents who were determined enough could compel their daughters to marry unwillingly.

It was, therefore, a white-faced Drusilla who returned to the parlour when summoned later in the day, where she found Sir Randal standing before the fireplace. He was looking towards the door as she entered, and stepped towards her, smiling. As she halted and held out her hand as though to ward him off, he stopped, puzzled.

"My love, what is it?" he asked in quick concern, and she almost broke down to hear the solicitude in his voice. Perhaps he did care for her, a little, she thought with a leaping heart, then firmly suppressed the hope, reminding herself of the fact that he was being forced to this, by his own honour and her father's threats. Only her own steadfast refusal could prevent it.

"You are ill? Tired? The journey was too hard for you? Oh, my dear Drusilla, we could have taken longer over it if you had but said!"

"We waited rather too long as it was, did we not?" she murmured, sinking down into a chair. "Yes, I am sorry, I am tired," she added, seizing on the excuse to explain her wan appearance.

"Then I will be brief, my love. Your father has given me permission to speak to you, and approves of what I have to ask. I do not wish him to sway you unduly, my love, for I hope and believe that you wish it for yourself. Drusilla, I want you so much, I have been hard put to it to wait so long before speaking to you. Will you marry me?"

Drusilla swallowed the lump in her throat. He sounded so sincere. It was so like him, she thought, to make the best of it, and try to pretend that it was what he had wished all along. He would not want her to realise that he was being forced into this action, but she must not accept the sacrifice. She could not deprive him of his true love.

"I thank you, Sir Randal," she managed to say at last. "You do me great honour, but I cannot accept."

"Cannot? Drusilla, I do not understand. You have not seemed indifferent to me. Have I mistaken your feelings?"

He came swiftly across the room and knelt beside her, taking her hand in his. She turned her face away to hide the expression in her eyes, which she knew would tell him how much she did indeed love him.

"I know that you offer only because of the damage to my reputation," she stammered. "That is nonsense, but my father will not believe it. No one we knew saw us, and Mistress Saddler will not talk, I am certain. Besides, what could it matter if it did become known to your friends?

I am not important to them, and my father can deny it if anyone here should accuse me!"

"What is all this?" he demanded, rising to his feet and pacing up and down. "Has your father told you that I offered for you because of those circumstances?"

Mutely she nodded, and he exclaimed in exasperation.

"I thought that he did not fully comprehend what I said," he commented. "Drusilla, my foolish little love, that is nonsense, as you so rightly say. I have loved you and wanted you since that day in Reading when I saw you so valiantly defending the little maid, Joan, against overwhelming odds! I would have spoken earlier, but a foolish sense of propriety made me wait until I could speak first with your father or brother. And see what has come of that! Drusilla, my offer has nought to do with our journey from Thornton Hall. I love you, as I have done for weeks past, and that is the only reason why I want to marry you!"

Drusilla was almost convinced, for he sounded so sincere, but she could not rid herself of the thought of Mary

Percy. Obviously, having determined on his course of action, Randal would not permit her to think that he was unwilling. He did not realise that she knew of his love for Mary, but to tell him that would, she considered, be pointless, for he would simply deny it. So she shook her head, and shrank away from him when he tried to take her hand again.

"I cannot marry you!" she gasped. "Please, Sir Randal, do not persist. There is a reason, a compelling reason, but I cannot — will not — tell you!"

At her physical avoidance of him he had drawn back, hurt and puzzled. Although she had never sought his caresses, she had not previously flinched from any contact, and had never rebuked him or struggled on the few occasions when he had been unable to restrain his ardour and had kissed her or held her hand. What could have changed in the short time since he had last seen her? Why should she regard him with such aversion now?

"Do you no longer trust me?" he asked quietly. "I had thought that we were friends, besides hoping that we might become lovers. Can you not tell me

cannot imagine that you will wish to remain when you learn what brings me!" he sneered.

"Explain yourself!" Randal snapped.

"Here? In a public room? You would not care for that, Sir Randal, for what I have to say is not to your credit!"

"Say what you will! You have no power to discredit me! What mischief do you intend?"

"No power? Have I none, indeed? Very well, then, and do not complain that I did not give you the opportunity to hear this in private!"

Randal glanced about him contemptuously. Apart from an old man snoring on a settle at the far end of the common room where they stood, there was no one in sight.

"I prefer not to be any more private with such as you," he said softly, "since that might lead people to believe we entertained feelings of friendship. Let all our dealings be public! I have no shame in them!"

Jacob flushed at his tone.

"You'll regret that," he promised, "when you're charged with murder!"

"Murder! What madness is this?" Randal asked with a surprised laugh.

"No madness." Jacob was beginning to enjoy himself. "I have obtained a confession from one of the fellows you wounded on the night Mistress Matthews died that it was you who caused her death!" he announced triumphantly.

"Mistress Matthews? Are you totally deranged? She died after a difficult and premature labour!"

"Contrived by the affray in her house."

"Caused by that, possibly, but how does that condemn me, apart from the mischance that I was the object of that cowardly attack?"

"You paid them to pretend to attack you, so that you might, in the confusion, murder Mistress Matthews," Jacob accused.

Randal stared at him in complete astonishment.

"You truly are insane," he commented, and turned to walk away.

Jacob was by now in full flow, however, and stepped hurriedly in front of him.

"No, you shall not escape until I have told you all we know! He — the man you wounded — says that you wished to have

190

poor Drusilla at your mercy. That was the reason you gave them."

"And the reason I killed or wounded them, too, I suppose," Randal said contemptuously.

"Of course, that was to destroy them for fear that they gave witness against you, as they have. You were not clever enough, Sir Randal! They escaped! But that is not all!"

"Indeed? What other fairy tale have you concocted?"

"No fairy tale. You prevented the midwife from attending Mistress Matthews. She swears that when she came, having been summoned by Drusilla, you threw her out of the house, and so Mistress Matthews died, as you had intended in the first place! Having failed to kill her in the fracas of the attack on the house, you saw to it that she did not receive the attention she needed!"

"You are being utterly ridiculous!" Randal exclaimed. "The midwife was a drunken, filthy wretch, and Mistress Matthews had better attention from the garrison surgeon than any she might have received from that old harridan. Whom do you think to convince with your ravings?"

"The surgeon, being in your pay, could easily have hastened Mistress Matthews' death, which the midwife, a respectable woman, would not have done!" Jacob continued, determined to have his full say.

"Pray take your story elsewhere!" Randal said impatiently. "Only a fool, knowing the facts, could give credence to it!"

"James is no fool!" Jacob said triumphantly.

"James Matthews?" Randal said, his eyebrows snapping together.

"Aye! That concerns you, I see! No doubt you were unaware of the fact that he is here in Devizes! You hoped to entrap Drusilla, having compromised her by your stratagems in pretending you were rescuing her from Parliament's army. Poor child! How could she, alone, resist you when you had her at your mercy, with another surgeon bribed to frighten her into remaining with you after she had been wounded — a mere scratch — by a stray bullet aimed by highwaymen."

Randal looked at him closely.

"What do you know of that business and Mistress Drusilla's injuries?" he asked sharply.

"I have heard it all! Never mind how I know! James has seen her! When she was inveigled away from Reading and I learned where she was being taken, I went to fetch her brother, and he is here now. He is with her."

"You knew that I proposed to bring her here, to her own parents, and say that she was in my power?" Randal asked mockingly.

"You could hardly keep her at your own home!" Jacob said quickly.

"Pray why not, if I had so desired it?"

"Because," Jacob paused, and then continued, blustering, "your family, your neighbours, would not have countenanced it. So you had to contrive to keep her elsewhere!"

"And arrange to shoot her, no doubt!"

"You would have invented some excuse. It is fortunate for you that James did not meet you in the street, for he is hot for vengeance. He would have raised a hue and cry!"

Randal surveyed him coolly, then turned on his heel and went up to his own bedchamber, leaving Mr Blagrave muttering triumphantly to himself at the thought that he had routed the enemy.

So that was the explanation of Drusilla's attitude when he had made his offer! thought Randal grimly. James had been to the house and must have told her of the false confession, and she had believed him! No wonder she had been so disturbed, had shrunk away from his touch. It was scarcely surprising that she would refuse to explain her reasons, if she truly believed him to be a murderer who had plotted to kill Elizabeth. The only wonder was that she had received him at all, and alone.

He wondered whether it would serve if he attempted to see her again, but came to the conclusion that she would most probably refuse to see him, or her parents, having learned of James' accusations, would forbid it. At last, he called for paper and writing materials, and wrote a short note saying that he had discovered the reason for her refusal and hoped, if he were permitted to see her again, to be able to convince her that it was not true. He could not bring himself to set down in writing even the mere suspicion that she might think him a murderer, for it was too painful to believe, and ended his brief epistle with the assurance that he loved her truly and always would.

Calling for a maid, he gave instructions for the immediate delivery of the sealed note, and by presenting her with a golden angel ensured her prompt compliance with the order. Randal waited impatiently for half an hour, and when the reply was brought to him tore open the missive.

Drusilla, weeping in her room, had been tempted almost beyond endurance to agree to see him again, but she knew that if she did she would weaken and accept his assurances that he did not love Mary Percy. Since she still believed that he would be denying his true love for a sense of honour which she could not think important, and making a sacrifice he would always regret, she had forced herself, after destroying two attempts which had been ruined by tell-tale tears falling on them, to write a brief refusal.

'Thank you for all that you have done to help me,' she wrote. 'I understand why you would seek to convince me, but my decision is made, and I cannot alter it. Please do not attempt to see me again, for that would give me too much pain; there is nought more to be said.'

Grim-faced, accepting that for the moment he had lost his love, Randal gave orders that he was to be roused early on the following morning, and had supper sent to him in his room. He was determined that he would return to Devizes and lay siege to Drusilla, but it seemed that for the moment she was so shocked by what she had been told that no good could come of forcing her to listen to him. In that event, he might as well travel on to Cornwall, and complete his mission there. Some time in the future he would return, and when the first shock and hurt was done with, Drusilla would begin to perceive the nonsense of the accusations against him, and he might yet win her.

8

EXHAUSTED by both the physical and emotional strains she had undergone, Drusilla pleaded illness and remained in her room. Apart from genuine weariness she feared that Randal, despite her note, would contrive to speak with her. Coming to see how she felt and tell her of James' arrival at suppertime, Mistress Matthews found her fast asleep, and left her in peace, so that it was morning before she learned of James' presence. Then, waking early, and despite her misery, feeling hungry, she descended to the dining parlour to find him and her father engaged in an acrimonious discussion.

James turned to her as she entered the room, and when she would have embraced him, exclaiming at his presence and telling him of her sorrow at Elizabeth's death, he thrust her away from him.

"Do not be a hypocrite!" he snapped. "You contributed to her death by your behaviour over that plaguey Royalist!"

"I?" she said, aghast. "James, what are you saying?"

"Do not pretend that you did not conspire with him so that she did not receive proper help!" he flung at her. "It was your doing that he ever came to the house, and I'd like to know more of that, too, for you do not appear to have been discreet! That a sister of mine should flaunt her association with the enemy disgusts me!"

"Sir Randal is not my enemy!" she protested, taken aback at his words.

"Are you now a Royalist?" he demanded.

"I am neither Royalist nor Parliamentarian!" she said angrily. "Sir Randal did his utmost to help Elizabeth, and but for him she would have been in greater distress!"

"Faugh! But for him she would not have suffered premature labour, when he deliberately feigned that fight, hoping that she would be killed in the fracas!"

"Deliberately? No, James, that is untrue!" she protested, shocked.

"I have ample proof, evidence from one of the men he hired to pretend that

198

attack. It was his misfortune that he did not kill them all, and they escaped to witness against him."

"I do not believe it!"

"You are besotted. He wanted you in his power, and thought that by disposing of Elizabeth while I was absent he would achieve it. The first attempt having failed, he sent away the midwife so that Elizabeth would have no help."

"That is untrue! The garrison surgeon attended to her, and was a deal more competent than that old hag who refused at first to come when I went to seek her help! As for the fight causing the premature labour, that may be true, but it was not Sir Randal's fault! He was the victim of it. Besides, Elizabeth had miscarried before — "

"As he knew!" James interposed. "You should have had more care for her, but you were so bent on your own grandiose plotting that she was a hindrance to you. And now I find that after all I have told him, father is still bent on your marrying the wretch!"

"But, James, you are distraught! What you say has not been proved!" his father said, distracted. "You were not there! It may be as Drusilla says! The confession may be false, a means of extorting money by a rogue who admits he is for hire to anyone who needs him!"

"I was not there, but my friend Blagrave was! He bears out what I have said. Indeed, but for him I would not have known the truth, but he sought out the rogue and forced him to confess! It cannot be a false confession since no money has been promised!"

"Jacob Blagrave!" Drusilla exclaimed. "He would do all he could to blacken Sir Randal's name, for his animosity is great!"

"He is jealous, I admit, for he knew that you favoured him until this Royalist came on the scene and bedazzled you with his Court manners and his title!"

"His title, yes," Mr Matthews said reflectively. "Indeed, James, it would be wrong to accuse him of this until he has had an opportunity of explaining it. He might be offended, and if in the circumstances he withdrew his offer for Drusilla, I doubt if I could bring him round to renewing it. He would consider it an adequate reason for evading such an unequal match."

"I am amazed that you could still contemplate marrying Drusilla to him!" James said in disgust. "The man's a murderer!"

"It is not proved, and it is an opportunity she would never have again!" his father pointed out. "Fancy my grandchildren having titles! A few generations ago we were simple yeomen, but my grandfather and father, and I myself, have laboured to amass riches and to rise in the world. Think what this would mean!"

James glared angrily at him.

"Father, you speak foolishly! What is a title? They can be bought if that is what you care for! For my part, I'd rather Drusilla wed an honest merchant like Blagrave than a titled rogue!"

"We do not have proof," Mr Matthews said pleadingly, clinging to his dreams of grandeur. "At least we should ask Sir Randal."

"There is proof enough for me, and Blagrave is here to tell you of it."

"Blagrave in Devizes?" Drusilla exclaimed in dismay, but James ignored her.

"We are fortunate that after all the scandal Drusilla has caused such a man is still willing to take her. He is wealthy, and will rise far. Already he has won the respect of the leading Parliamentarians in Reading, and since the outcome of the war is now certain he will rise even higher, while your precious Sir Randal is like to lose his title as well as his lands!"

"I will never wed Jacob Blagrave!" Drusilla announced loudly. "And you need not quarrel over Sir Randal, for I have seen him and told him that I cannot accept his offer. There is no fear that I will marry either of them!"

"Not accept? What is this? You wicked girl, why?" her father demanded, astounded.

"I saw him yesterday afternoon and told him."

"Oh, then all is lost, for he will never renew his offer!" Mr Matthews cried in despair. "He made it only from a sense of honour, and if it had not been for that he would never have stooped to wed a girl from our rank in life! Daughter, what have you done? I should have accepted on your behalf!"

"You must have come to know his character better," James commented slowly, ignoring his father's lamentations and looking with more favour on Drusilla. "No doubt you discovered his real disposition when he thought he had you in his power. Thank your good fortune that you have escaped, and that Mr Blagrave is prepared to overlook this escapade."

"Why did you refuse?" her father demanded.

Goaded into a truthful reply, Drusilla said, through gritted teeth:

"Because he does not love me! He loves someone else, and was forced to offer for me because of the misfortune we met with on the journey here! But for that he would never have considered it!"

"Loves someone else? What is that to the point?" Mr Matthews demanded. "So you still have your romantic notions? I do not understand you, but it appears that you have wilfully thrown away the best opportunity you are likely to get! And if it becomes generally known that you spent a week alone with him you will receive no more offers! You had best be thankful Mr Blagrave is willing to overlook it. Oh, well, I suppose it was ridiculous for me to dream that it could possibly happen!"

For some time longer Drusilla had to endure her father's lamentations and her brother's predictions of what would happen to her if she again repulsed Mr Blagrave. James had still not entirely absolved her from blame in Elizabeth's death, and when he saw that further argument about Drusilla's affairs was at the moment unproductive, he turned to questioning her closely about the events in Reading during the siege, and particularly how it had affected Elizabeth. It seemed that he had a morbid fascination in lingering over all the distressing details of Elizabeth's death, and in having to recall them and describe them to him again and again, Drusilla suffered intensely during the next few weeks.

She had heard no more of Randal. He had disappeared completely the day after having made her the offer and been rejected.

"He went after Mr Blagrave encountered him at the Crown, and told him of our suspicions," James reported to her when he was in an unusually benign mood. "I could have wished otherwise, but no matter, for when the fighting is done, and if he has not been killed, I will hunt him down and bring him to justice. He left in considerable haste, I am told, so he was obviously frightened."

"Frightened? You delude yourself if you think Sir Randal would ever be afraid, especially of a windbag like Jacob Blagrave!" Drusilla retorted.

Mr Blagrave remained in Devizes to torment her further by persisting in his courtship. He told Drusilla that he was there to do business with the woollen merchants, braving the small local Royalist garrison in the town, for Parliament wished to encourage the trade, so necessary for prosperity and the consequent payment of taxes, and apparently Mr Blagrave had some special commission from them. Despite Drusilla's coldness and repeated refusals to listen to him, he blandly assumed that eventually she would succumb, or be forced to marry him.

During these weeks Drusilla's only consolation was to escape from the town and renew her friendship with Tom Copley. She roamed over the downs with him, and sometimes Tom's young brother George, who lived with him in a small cottage at the foot of Beacon Hill, came with them. At these times her misery was partially dulled, although she thought she would never regain contentment after the glimpse of happiness that she had been shown. It was only for brief moments that she forgot Sir Randal, for she was constantly reliving all their times together, or wondering what had become of him, and whether he had yet returned from Cornwall to Thornton Hall and married Mary Percy.

News of the war came slowly to Devizes, but Drusilla took little interest apart from wondering where Sir Randal was. She did not care about the fortifying of London that was continuing, or the news from the north where the Royalists were having some successes. When news of Hopton's victory at Stratton came in the middle of May, she cared only to wonder for the hundredth time whether Randal had completed his mission and left Cornwall. The intelligence that Lord Essex had penetrated to within five miles of Oxford was more worrying, but it was a solitary effort, and soon tales of the exploits of Prince Rupert filtered through, mainly of his daring raids on Parliamentary outposts between Oxford and London. Drusilla thought back with wonder to the time when she had met this man about whom marvellous stories crediting him with almost magical powers were beginning to be told.

James was more concerned for events in the west, and when he heard that Waller was leaving the siege of Worcester in an attempt, vain, as it happened, to prevent the forces of Hopton, Lord Hertford, and Prince Maurice from joining together, he departed from Devizes to rejoin the army.

June passed. With James' departure Drusilla felt less threatened, for she could withstand Jacob Blagrave's entreaties by ignoring them, or patiently repeating that she had no intention of agreeing to wed him. Her father occasionally berated her for a fool, but she was never sure whether he referred to her loss of Randal or refusal of Blagrave, and she did not care sufficiently to argue, knowing that it could have no effect. Only from her mother did she feel she received some sympathy, for Mistress Matthews, perturbed at her daughter's utter want of spirits, sought to comfort her in little ways. She was too much afraid of her husband, though, to insist that he send Mr Blagrave away, and she secretly hoped that eventually his continued devotion might bring Drusilla to appreciate and accept him. Realising that the escapes on to the downs, and the rides and walks with Tom Copley helped Drusilla to remain calm, she contrived to keep these secret from her husband, often saying, when he asked where Drusilla was, that she had sent her on some errand, and warning Drusilla not to allow her father to know where she had been.

On the first Thursday of July, Drusilla was in the market buying butter when she heard a man nearby excitedly telling a small crowd news of a recent battle.

"Near Bath, it were," he was saying, "on Tuesday. The Cornish won, as they did at Stratton, by running straight up the side of a steep hill. I do hear that they have marvellous steep hills in Cornwall and

Devon, but they must breed special men! I'd not be able to run up Beacon Hill, and these by all accounts be steeper!"

"The King won?" someone asked worriedly. "What will that do to our trade?"

"Well, he may have won, but he did not have it all his own way," the news-carrier said slowly. "Sir Bevil Grenvile, and several others of the Cornish leaders, were killed, and since men won't easily go out of their own counties, and it was only for him and Hopton that they left Cornwall behind, no doubt they'll go back. I hear Sir William Waller is still strong enough to be chasing them back after he brought his men together again."

Drusilla experienced some concern then for James. She had been so lost in her own misery that she had given little thought to his possible danger, but now she realised that he was liable to be killed or wounded, and she wished that they had not been so deeply at odds when he had left Devizes.

On the following day, they heard that the two armies were moving eastwards from Bath, and the Royalists had halted at Chippenham, ten miles distant, on their way to try and join with the King at Oxford.

"When they have gone past, James will be able to come and visit us again," Mistress Matthews said, pleased at the prospect of seeing her son.

On Saturday, there was no further news, and on Sunday, to escape a promised visit from Jacob Blagrave, Drusilla had her mare saddled and rode out on to the downs. She found Tom, sitting under a clump of trees and whittling away at a piece of wood that he quickly turned into an astonishingly lifelike replica of a rabbit, a family of which were playing happily a short distance away in a small hollow.

She sat beside him, while her mare was content to crop the short, springy turf, and listened as he talked of the rabbits, telling her how, long ago, when he was a small boy, he had brought a baby rabbit that had been lost back to his father's small cottage, which he now lived in himself, and reared it.

"It were a mistake, Mistress Drusilla,"

he concluded wistfully. "I tried to send him back to the downs when he grew old enough to feed for himself, but he had forgotten the dangers, and a fox got him the first night. I could hear him screaming, not far from the hut, but I was too late. The next day I found the trail of blood where the fox had carried him off."

Drusilla shuddered.

"Poor little rabbit. I suppose he was too trusting."

"Aye. It might have been better to have left him to die when he was a baby, instead of letting him enjoy life only to lose it."

Drusilla thought of her own lost love. Would she have preferred never to have met Randal?

"No!" she said suddenly and vehemently. "It is better to have something, even if only for a short while, than never to have had it at all! I'd rather experience both joy and sorrow than never have either."

Tom smiled at her understandingly. She had never talked to him of Randal, but he seemed to have an instinct for her moods, and she felt that he was by nature wise.

"The joy might return," he consoled. "And if it does not the sorrow will lessen. Even the rabbit suffered but a little while."

After some time, during which they said nothing more, Drusilla stood up.

"I must go," she said, looking across at the sun which was beginning to drop lower in the sky. "I must not be late for supper, or father will demand to know what I have been doing."

He nodded, and seemed totally absorbed in his carving. As she mounted and rode off he did not speak or even look after her. He was so contented, needing no one else, and as she rode along the western crest of the hills Drusilla envied him.

Below her, the plain spread out, marshy in parts, and dotted with several villages. As Drusilla reached the point where she would have to turn left to ride round the top of a deep ravine, she paused and looked back. Suddenly something caught her attention, and she narrowed her eyes, shading them against the glare of the sun. Below her, on the road leading from the village of Netherstreet, there was considerably more activity than might have been expected on a Sunday afternoon.

A long column of marching men were approaching Devizes, those at the front marching in apparent good order, but at the rear there was considerable confusion, and many horsemen galloping about. After a few moments, Drusilla perceived that the rear of the column was being attacked, and as she watched, wondering which army was which, she saw a detachment at the rear of the column halt and turn to face their attackers. They had chosen to halt at a ford about a mile out of the town, near the village of Rowde, and Drusilla soon saw that they were endeavouring to deflect the attack from the main body, which was making as much speed as possible towards the town.

On realising that which ever army it was there would soon be soldiers in Devizes, and not wishing to experience again the alarums of Reading, Drusilla turned her horse and made the best speed she could through Roundway village and along the lane which led past St Mary's

Church towards her home.

Already the news had reached the town, and after taking her mare along the small back roads to the stables, Drusilla went through the house to the front to peer out of the parlour window at the crowds milling about in the Market Place. From the comments she heard it appeared that the Royalist army had marched from Chippenham, and the townsfolk, fearful of the trouble that was likely to be brought upon them, were helplessly discussing what to do.

Suddenly there was a knock on the door, and it was repeated with frantic haste long before any of the maids could go to open it. When it was opened, Drusilla heard her father coming from the small room he used as an office, and addressing the new arrival, asking in what way he could be of service.

Jacob Blagrave, stuttering in his nervousness, replied.

"Mr Matthews, you have always b-been kind. I must leave Devizes, I c-cannot stay! I am a known supporter of P-Parliament! They will k-kill me, but my horse has gone lame, and that wretched

214

innkeeper will not lend me another! There is nowhere I c-can go, or I would not trouble you, but I b-beg you, assist me now! Lend me a horse!"

Drusilla opened the door and went out into the hall.

"Running away, Mr Blagrave?" she enquired sweetly, animated for a while at this evidence of his pusillanimity. He glared at her and straightened his shoulders a little.

"I wish to join Sir William Waller, and f-fight!" he managed to say. "There is no point in remaining here, to be thrown into some stinking cell, and t-tortured!"

"No point whatsoever," she agreed cordially. "Father, I beg of you, do help Mr Blagrave to leave Devizes!"

Mr Matthews, anxious to rid himself of a visitor who might prove a danger if the Royalists were bent on vengeance, hastily agreed and led Jacob off through the house. The man was so fearful that he did not even remember to bid Drusilla farewell, and she, a contemptuous smile on her lips, watched him go, hoping that it was the last she would see of him.

She returned to the window, and

gradually the townsfolk, realising that they could do nothing, drifted back to their homes as the first of the Royalist foot entered the town, congregating in the Market Place until dispositions could be made.

Called by her mother to a somewhat belated supper, Drusilla left her vantage post. The whole family were eating this meal when a peremptory knock came on the door. One of the maids, with a startled look at her master, rose to go and answer it, but Mr Matthews laid down his napkin and motioned her back on to her stool.

"I will go," he said, and went slowly to the door, leaving the door from the dining parlour open so that the conversation could be heard.

"Mr Matthews?"

"Indeed, sir. What may I do for you?"

"I beg your pardon, sir, but I've orders to quarter myself and four of my troopers in your house. I'm told you have sufficient stabling for their horses?"

"I — this is an imposition, sir! I cannot agree!" Mr Matthews protested.

"Begging your pardon, sir, but 'tis not in your power to refuse. The men must be

"He didn't say, sir."

"Then I will come this evening. Pray tell him that I desire to speak with him, and will return this evening."

He left the house, for he did not consider it would advance his cause to speak with Drusilla's mother. Her father had seemed in favour of the match, yet had told her that Randal was in honour bound to make his offer. He must attempt to remove that impression, and at the same time discover what it was that Drusilla was so concerned about. Until he knew that, it did not seem that anyone other than Mr Matthews would be able to assist him.

Thoughtful, speculating on what Drusilla's reason could be, he crossed the market place and walked slowly along St John's Street until he came to the Crown. Turning into the main entrance, his abstraction left him suddenly as he came face to face with Jacob Blagrave.

"You!" he ejaculated. "What in the world do you do in Devizes?"

Jacob smiled unpleasantly.

"I have more right here than you, Sir Randal Thornton, and more success! I what is troubling you? I might be able to explain it if, as I hope, there is some misunderstanding. At least give me the opportunity of trying, my dearest one."

"No, I cannot! Oh, pray, do not beg it of me! I shall always be grateful to you for the help you have given me, and think of you kindly, but there must not — I cannot — see you ever again, and as for marriage! It is unthinkable!"

He made another attempt to persuade her to reveal what was troubling her, but she became so distressed that he desisted, and said that he hoped to speak with her father later in the day, then, Drusilla having regained enough control to bid him farewell and a safe journey, he left the parlour.

One of the maids was hovering about outside, and he asked abruptly where he could find Mr Matthews.

"Oh, sir, he's gone to visit someone. I cannot say who. Mr James has also come home today! He came after you left before, sir, and now he has gone off with the master!"

"Mr James? Do you know when your master will have returned?"

quartered, and all houses will have to take their share. Indeed, your house seems so large I'd not be surprised if you were not told to take more than five! But it was the Colonel's own orders, and he picked on your house and sent me straight here before you could be bothered with anyone else. He told me to bring four of the most reliable men, and see that you and your family were troubled as little as possible. We'll most like be gone in a day or two, sir," he added persuasively.

Mr Matthews continued to protest, maintaining that he had not sufficient room for five extra people.

"No doubt we'll all be a trifle squeezed," the other replied. "But if you don't permit us to establish ourselves now, methinks you'll have to take more, and less well-conducted men, later!"

Reluctantly, Mr Matthews saw the sense of this, and indicated that he might step inside.

"The stable yard can be reached from the side. Ben," he called, beckoning the stable lad from the table, "come and show them the way and see that they know where to put their horses."

Mistress Matthews had been watching the soldier, and she noticed the way in which he kept averting his eyes from the appetising food spread on the table. Her motherly heart was touched.

"When you've stabled the horses, come and join us at supper," she offered, "for I doubt if you're fed properly in camp!"

He laughed, embarrassed.

"It looks good," he complimented her. "We don't fare so badly, but we've been on the march since noon, and it looks tempting!"

The five troopers were soon seated at the table, somewhat shy and full of gratitude for the welcome Mistress Matthews had extended to them. The leader and two of the men were in their late thirties, all family men, who spoke longingly of their desire to be done with the fighting and return home to their wives and children. The others were father and son, the latter no more than sixteen, who had no family apart from each other, and were content to be professional soldiers. The father had served in Europe for some years, and the son hoped to go there after they had finished with the rebels, a task all of them considered would be a short one.

After they had eaten, their leader, who introduced himself as Sergeant Cox, announced that he must report to the Colonel. The others, after profuse thanks for the hospitality, took themselves off to the two rooms which had been allocated to them, and left the family alone to speculate on this turn of events.

All night, there was considerable noise and activity in the town, as the Cornish infantry and the cavalry led by Prince Maurice and Lord Hertfort poured into the town, many of the men unable to find accommodation for either themselves or their horses, and having to make the best of bivouacking in the streets. On the following day there was still considerable confusion, with items of news trickling through to the Matthews family who, obeying the advice of the friendly Sergeant Cox, had remained indoors.

They learned from the other troopers, who were content to sit and rest after their exertions, of the carnage at the battle of Lansdown, and the loss of several gallant leaders, amongst them Sir Bevil

Grenvile. There was also the later disaster when Lord Hopton had been injured by a wagon of powder exploding near him, rendering him blind so that he had been carried to Devizes on a litter, while the cavalry had held off the attacks of Waller's men all the way from Chippenham.

In the afternoon, Drusilla was again sitting by the window, watching the ceaseless activity outside, when her attention was caught by two officers riding past on the far side of the Market Place. The first thing to strike her was the keen attention one of the riders appeared to be paying to her own house, and after a closer scrutiny she rose to her feet in excitement, for it was Sir Randal.

"Oh, he is not dead!" was her first exclamation, and she was about to lean from the window to attract his attention when doubts seized her, and instead she drew back behind the curtains from where she could watch without being seen.

She had recalled that she had sent a very definite refusal to him in reply to his own letter, and in her later musings on the affair, she had realised that her mention of the insuperable reason, which she could not explain, for that refusal, might have been taken by him to refer to the accusations of Jacob Blagrave. She had reasoned that, since Jacob had seen him and told him of the accusations as soon as he had returned to the Crown, and there had been time for James to tell her also before she saw Sir Randal, (although in fact she had not known of it until afterwards,) Randal could have assumed that it was these accusations which caused her refusal. If he thought she believed him to have contrived Elizabeth's murder, he would most certainly not wish to renew his acquaintance with her, apart from the embarrassment consequent upon his reluctant offer of marriage, and the relief he must feel at having been refused. She was nevertheless hurt to think that he might believe that she accepted the accusations, and although she knew that it was impossible, and she still would not tell him the real reason for her refusal, she longed to set him straight on the matter.

So thinking, she watched as he rode slowly along, turning occasionally to reply to a remark of his companion, whom

Drusilla belatedly recognised as Prince Rupert.

The two men disappeared from sight as they turned into the road leading to the castle, and Drusilla blinked back her tears. Almost she wished that she had not seen Randal, for it revived with fierce intensity her despair at the loss of her love. She knew that she could never love any other man, and recoiled in horror at the occasional references by her mother to her marriage.

Mistress Matthews, beginning to realise that Drusilla was implacably opposed to Jacob Blagrave, and not accepting her husband's gloomy view that Drusilla had destroyed all hope of a respectable match by her behaviour, had started to think of men who might overlook her former capricious attitude, and be willing to wed a beautiful, as well as amply dowered girl. Drusilla refused utterly to contemplate any of the suggestions her mother put forward, saying that she had no desire or intention of marrying, so that between her husband's pessimism and her daughter's lack of interest, Mistress Matthews was deeply distressed, for the prospect of her lovely daughter remaining unwed was to her a matter of disgrace and shame.

Hoping for another glimpse of Sir Randal, Drusilla barely left the window all day, but he did not reappear. Sergeant Cox came back and was closeted with his men for some time, afterwards departing again towards the castle. At suppertime he announced that the Matthews were to lose their uninvited guests.

"We ride out tonight," he told them. "There is too little room in the town for all the cavalry, and it has been decided to remove us."

"But has not Waller surrounded the town?" Mr Matthews asked, puzzled. "I have seen for myself his troops drawn up on the slopes of Roundway Hill, and I am told he has encircled the town, intending to attack."

Sergeant Cox nodded.

"Aye, he might attack, but it is impossible to circle the town completely because of the marshes and lack of sufficient men. I do not anticipate great difficulty for a compact group of horsemen to break through their lines. Not with Prince Maurice and men like my own

Colonel at the head of them!" he added with considerable pride.

The men retired after supper to make their preparations, and to get what rest they could, but there was no possibility of sleep for Drusilla. Outside in the Market Place, long before midnight, the cavalry began to assemble, but although she watched eagerly, in the uncertain light given by a few flares she could not distinguish Randal's features.

One of the last to join the assembly was Sergeant Cox, who sent out his men and turned to express his gratitude to Mistress Matthews for all she had done.

"We do not often meet with such kindness from those we are forced to incommode," he said ruefully. "I'm truly grateful to Colonel Thornton for sending us here. I thought that you were friends of his, and he has asked how you did, although it seems he has been too occupied with other matters to visit you. I'll certainly tell him how royally you have treated us."

He was gone, and Drusilla turned away and went swiftly to her room to ponder what he had said, and escape the puzzled looks her mother was casting her. So Randal had been responsible for ensuring that decent, sober men had been sent to their house! He must care for her a little! Why had she not guessed that it had been his actions, for who else could have known of them and been so thoughtful? Briefly a flicker of hope rose in her breast, but it soon died as she thought of Mary Percy, and reminded herself that he had made no attempt to see her. She did not believe that military duties could have kept him busy every single moment, and if he had wished to he would have snatched at least a few minutes with her. No, he had simply acted generously, ensuring that they had been as little troubled as possible. Mayhap he recalled the annoyances she had experienced in Reading, and wished to spare her a repetition of them, even though he did not care sufficiently to make an attempt to see her himself. It was courtesy on his part, and nothing more.

The sounds of the cavalry died away, and Drusilla wondered where they were bound for. They were vastly outnumbered by Waller's men, so could hardly be planning to attack him from the rear. So far as she knew there were no other Royalists near at hand, although it was difficult to know what to believe, for the news they received was so vague, and often contradicted the following day, and they could not be going to fetch help. They must have determined on escaping to save the cavalry, since otherwise all would be taken, and leaving the Cornish infantry to their fate. Devizes would soon be overrun with Waller's men, James probably amongst them. It was only that which permitted Drusilla to look forward to the next few days with any degree of calm. He would surely protect them from the sort of outrages she had witnessed in Reading. However, it was not the contemplation of this possibility that caused the tears to flow that night before Drusilla, exhausted by her emotions, at last fell asleep.

9

ON the following day, the soldiers left in the town, between two and three thousand of them, were intensely busy. They continued to block all the ways into the town by digging ditches, or blocking the lanes with huge trunks of trees and anything else which could be obtained. Any other means of defence was pointless, since the small and inadequate earthworks round the edge of the town would not serve to halt a determined advance.

It had earlier been discovered that the Royalists were short of match, and Mistress Matthews was indignant when she was forced to give up all the bed cord in the house.

"What in the world can they want with that?" she demanded of her husband when they sat at dinner.

"They plan to beat it and boil it in resin to make match," he replied wearily. "They are stripping the roofs of lead for bullets, but I hear that they have only two barrels of powder left, so it will be to no avail."

"Sergeant Cox told me that they were expecting some powder to arrive," Drusilla offered.

"No, it has been captured, I hear, by Waller. He intercepted a force of Royalists early this morning," her father said.

"Why does not Waller attack?" Drusilla wondered. "He has so many more men. From the attic windows I have seen the thousands drawn up on the slopes above Roundway, and yet all he does is fire on the town occasionally."

"No doubt he is afeard," one of the maids contributed. "My brother told me that he was almost captured last night, when some of the King's men came across his supper, left uneaten in a farmhouse at Roundway!"

"How could they get there?" Mistress Matthews asked, puzzled. "Surely they cannot ride in and out at will?"

"It would not be difficult, methinks," Mr Matthews replied. "Although Waller has so many more men he must spread them more thinly to try and surround the town, and they would not be difficult to evade, particularly in the darkness."

All that day the Parliamentary troops could be seen on the hillsides overlooking the town while the Royalists continued their limited preparations for defence. During the afternoon, there was a lull while, with some of Waller's troops having cautiously penetrated to the outskirts of the town, he offered to intercede for the Royalists with Parliament if they surrendered.

"Think your Lord Hopton will surrender?" Drusilla asked her father, as both of them watched from the highest windows of the house.

"He must," was his reply. "There is no reason in holding out, for Waller must eventually succeed. Let us hope that before they conclude they do as little damage to our town as possible!"

However, it seemed as though Hopton would not surrender. The bombardment began again later in the evening and continued until darkness, when the attackers withdrew to the hills to be secure from any sallies from the town, and the citizens speculated on what relief the Royalists could expect.

On Wednesday morning, Drusilla woke to the sound of heavy rain against her shutters, and the bombardment that morning was as a result a mild affair. As the rain eased later in the day another attack was launched, and some furious fighting ensued.

Mistress Matthews, having at first been terrified, had now developed a curious fatalism, and having very sensibly concluded that there was little any of them could do either to affect the outcome or determine the results to themselves, she set the maids and Drusilla on to sorting through the linen and setting aside that which needed mending.

Drusilla was in one of the bedrooms at the back of the house when there was a terrified scream from Betty. Drusilla dropped the pile of sheets she was replacing in a press and ran to discover what had happened.

Betty was clinging to the window frame, and pointing excitedly.

As Drusilla ran across to her, she saw out of the window a small troop of horsemen gallop furiously out of the

Brittox and across the Market Place, flourishing their swords as they went.

"'Tis the rebels! They will be on us! Oh, Mistress, save me!" Betty moaned, and screamed again when another, larger troop went hurtling after the first.

"Pull yourself together, Betty!" Drusilla advised. "And you had best not permit my father to hear you call them rebels, for remember Mr James is with them!"

"What will they do to us, Mistress Drusilla?" the girl asked.

"Why, nought, I trust, once they have driven out the Royalists. I suppose we shall have to endure more soldiers quartered on us, but when my brother comes, as he is certain to do, he will ensure that we are treated courteously, so you need have no fears."

Betty did not seem reassured, but she forbore to scream again, and the two girls watched several more of the Parliamentary troops ride at full gallop through the town, fired on occasionally by a hidden musketeer. Then, after this brief surge of activity, an odd silence fell and no more soldiers were to be seen.

Suppertime came, and it was discovered

that Ben was missing. As Mistress Matthews was making anxious enquiries, discovering from the other servants that he had not been seen for at least two hours, the culprit slid in through the kitchen door, failing completely in his obvious desire to be unobtrusive.

"Where have you been?" Mr Matthews demanded, and Ben had to confess that, against orders, he had crept out into the town to try and discover what was happening.

"They are parleying!" he announced, and this news caused so much comment and speculation that Ben was able to join the suppertable and begin to eat before anyone could chastise him for his disobedience. Beyond saying that he would be most severely punished if he again disobeyed orders, Mr Matthews ignored it.

No more firing was heard that night, but on the following morning it was clear to the townsfolk that Waller did not intend to prevaricate any longer. His forces were drawn up in full strength on the slopes of Roundway Hill, and it was obvious even to those who had no military knowledge that he was preparing for a major attack. The Royalists in the town, heavily outnumbered, made preparations for a forlorn defence, the sound of cannonfire suddenly boomed from the north-east, behind the Parliamentary army, from the direction of the downs.

Ben, too excited to heed Mr Matthews' orders, again went into the town to glean news. When he returned, even Mr Matthews was too astonished at what he had discovered to utter a reprimand.

"The soldiers are saying that it's relief from Oxford, that the cavalry went to fetch!" he announced.

"From Oxford? Why, they must have ridden near a hundred miles!" Mr Matthews exclaimed.

"It cannot be," his wife protested. "Almost a hundred miles in less than three days? They left on Tuesday, before daybreak, and would have had no sleep that night!"

"Some of the leaders think it a trick to draw them out of the town," Ben went on, "though Hopton urges them to go."

"The Parliament men are moving

away!" Betty ran down the stairs at that moment to report, and they all accompanied her back to the attics from where they could watch as Waller and his men marched away from the town, to draw up again facing across the downs on the summit of Roundway Hill.

"Is it a ruse?" Mr Matthews wondered, but Drusilla was thinking only of Randal, who might at that moment be approaching by the same roads over which they had ridden so many weeks ago. If the rumour was correct, it seemed inevitable that a battle would be fought, and her brother and her loved one would both be involved, but on opposing sides. She twisted her hands together in agony, and unable to listen calmly to the excited speculations of her parents and the servants, went to sit in her room where they would not witness the fear in her eyes.

There was no more firing of cannon to be heard during the long afternoon, and Ben reported that the Cornishmen had not moved out of the town, despite the disappearance of Waller from the ridge, for fear that it was an ambush and they would find Waller lying in wait for them just beyond Roundway Hill.

Some time later the sound of cheering in the Market Place brought Drusilla to the window. She saw the Cornish infantry gathering, and having formed into companies, march out of the town along the Roundway road. It appeared from the shouts of triumph she heard that a victory had been won by Royalist cavalry from Oxford, and on receiving this intelligence, the more timid officers had finally agreed to leave the shelter of the town.

After they had gone, the townsfolk poured on to the streets to discuss the events of the siege and this amazing battle which had taken place out of their sight on the downs. Drusilla came out, too, for after having kept close to the house since Sunday night she was anxious alike for air and news.

A few Royalist cavalry had by now reached Devizes, some wounded, others carrying or giving assistance to those more seriously hurt. One soldier, relinquishing his injured comrade to the ministrations of a couple of motherly women who clucked sympathetically over his plight, leaned against his horse and stared about him. Drusilla, desperate for news, approached tentatively.

"What happened?" she asked. "We heard that the Royalists won a magnificent victory."

He surveyed her for a moment before replying, then nodded.

"Aye, and no thanks to the Cornishmen, who stayed safely in hiding till all was done for them!"

"I think they feared a trap," Drusilla explained, but he snorted in disbelief.

"Poltroons!" he exclaimed.

"But what happened? You came from Oxford?"

"Aye. Prince Maurice and some of the officers rode in on Tuesday morning, when none of us knew what had become of them, only that there had been a crushing defeat at Lansdown."

"But Lansdown was a victory for us!" Drusilla cried, unconsciously ranging herself on the side of the Royalists.

"So we know now, but some fools who ran away before the end of the battle did not halt until they reached Oxford, and it was their lying tales we heard! It was not until Prince Maurice himself arrived that we knew the truth."

"And you rode back here?"

"Aye, less than two thousand of us. Sir John Byron and Lord Wilmot came, and Prince Maurice and some others, despite their long ride, insisted on coming back as volunteers. We had but cavalry, for 'twas too far to march infantry in time, and we expected help from the Cornish foot! Twice our strength, Waller had, and still we beat him! We came up over a hill to see him waiting for us, and then we charged! Oh, how we charged at them! We near split open Hazelrig's Lobsters, despite their armour. Have you seen any?" he demanded.

Drusilla shook her head.

"Covered in plate, they are, so tight they can hardly move! We dealt with them, and then with Waller on the other wing, and they turned and fled! Only the foot stood, and 'tis my belief that's only because they did not know where to go with the town to their backs! However, before we'd finished them off, my sergeant was hurt by a pike, and I brought him down here."

Drusilla was about to ask him if Sir Randal Thornton had been engaged in the fight when she felt an insistent tug on the sleeve of her gown. Looking round she saw George Copley, Tom's young brother, and he put his finger to his lips and beckoned her away. Leaving the soldier to tell his tale to the small crowd that had collected about him, she followed George behind a wagon.

"What is it?" she asked, puzzled, for she had never seen him in the town before.

"Tom, he said I was to come and fetch 'ee," he whispered, looking all about him in fright that someone might overhear.

"Fetch me? Where? Why?" she demanded.

"To our cottage," he replied, obviously considering such a query foolish. "Tom said I was to tell 'ee James was there, hurt bad."

"James?" Drusilla exclaimed. "Oh, how badly?"

George shrugged. "Tom says he'll most like live. Not like the other."

"What other?" she demanded, but George shook his head.

"Tom said to come quick," was all he would say.

"I'll come, of course, but ought I not to bring my father as well? James will need to be carried home, and my father can arrange for that."

George shook his head impatiently.

"Tom said I was to tell no one else, Mistress Drusilla! He said Master James shouldn't be moved awhile, but he was calling so wild like for 'ee, and so Tom said best fetch 'ee, but not to tell anyone else. 'Twere Master James, seemingly, that wanted it kept secret," he added. "He didn't like it when Tom said to fetch Master Matthews, said he weren't to be told, yet."

"I'll get my mare and you can ride pillion," Drusilla decided swiftly, and turned to lead the way along the side road to the stables. As there was no time to change into a riding habit she thought that she could manage better without a saddle, and so after she had bridled the mare she led her quickly outside. Hitching up her skirts as she had done many times before, she scrambled on to the mare's back and George, delighted at

239

this rare opportunity of riding, quickly climbed up behind her. They set off, avoiding the main streets, and making for the road that led to Netherstreet, below the shoulder of the hills, and close to Tom's cottage.

She had some difficulty in manoeuvring past the obstacles set up to hinder Waller's advance, but finally found a place where an upturned wagon had been pulled aside, obviously by the cavalry which had penetrated into the town on the previous day, and was soon trotting along the track away from the town, with attention to spare to question George.

"There were a mighty battle on the downs," he told her. "Tom and I were on Beacon Hill with the sheep, and we saw both armies coming across from Roughridge and Roundway, to meet in the dip in the centre. First one charged, then the other, and then the first again. I never seen nought like it."

"What of James?" she asked.

"Tom found him. When the battle were over, they tried to run away, most of 'em, and came right past us, making for Chippenham way. But the hill was steeper

240

than they thought, and many of the horses fell, and rolled down the slopes, over and over and over. Some of 'em turned to the north, and got away, because 'tis flatter there, but those that turned towards Devizes were in worse case."

Drusilla shuddered, and nodded in agreement as she looked to her right where the steep slopes of the hills rose up to the downs. There were many ravines in the sides of the hills, and it was no place to take a horse, even if there were no need for haste.

"What happened?" she asked, but could see part of the answer for herself in the terrible carnage of dead bodies and the corpses of horses strewn about the slopes.

"Master James knows the land, and he tried to make for the old sheep road, where 'tis less steep," George answered, "but there were so many, all so frantic to get away, that he was caught in the rush and fell, and some horse rolled over him and broke his leg. He'll be fit again soon, Tom said, so don't fret, Mistress Drusilla," he added, and Drusilla reflected that if James had to break his leg she'd as soon he did it where Tom could care for him, and set it again, as anywhere else. Tom, with that instinct often possessed by those who lived close to nature, could doctor any animal, and set both animal and human bones better than most surgeons.

"Tom and I were going back to the cottage," George continued, "when we came across Master James. Lying at the bottom of a small slope, he were, where he'd rolled, and lucky to be there, for he'd been thrown out of the way of the rest. There were another man there, but he was worse, and after Tom had carried Master James to the cottage he sent me to fetch you, saying that he'd go back to see if the other were still alive, though he doubted it. Tom said he were too badly hurt."

Drusilla was asking more questions to try and discover whether James had any other injuries, when suddenly a man stepped from behind some bushes, brandishing a sword. Drusilla's mare reared at the unexpected apparition, and though Drusilla contrived to keep her seat, George slid to the ground.

"I'll take the horse," the man said curtly. "Down you get, my girl!"

He had grasped the reins, and though Drusilla struggled, she was no match for him and he soon pulled her to the ground. She struck at him with the whip she carried, but the slight cut she inflicted merely angered him. Twisting the reins about one arm, he seized Drusilla and pulled her to him.

"You're a tasty armful, and no mistake. I like spirited lasses," he commented, and bent to kiss her.

Struggling to evade him, she screamed, but he chuckled and tightened his grip.

"They're all too busy or too dead to care," he said callously. "Have pity on a poor soldier! Two weeks it is that I've been fighting or marching, and barely a glimpse have I had of a cuddlesome wench like you! Now I've got me a fresh horse to carry me away from this plaguey town, I'll take some pleasure first, whether you will or no!"

At that moment, George, rising from his tumble, came rushing to Drusilla's assistance, but the man kicked out at him and with a yelp of pain George fell

243

to the ground, winded. Dragging Drusilla with him, the man contrived to hitch the mare's reins to the low branch of a tree, and then he turned to her, surveying her in growing appreciation.

"Aye, you'll be worth stopping for," he commented, and with a sudden twist of his arm, pulled both Drusilla's hands behind her back. He tied a kerchief round them, and then left her for a moment while he did the same for George, still writhing on the ground from the blow he had received. Then the man came back to Drusilla, and began to drag her, resisting furiously, towards the bushes from which he had first appeared.

Drusilla had been working to free her hands from the somewhat insecurely tied knots that bound them, and just as he reached the bushes she got them free, and with a cry of rage tried to claw at his face. Startled, he backed away, and then, with a savage laugh, seized one arm and twisted it cruelly, laughing louder as Drusilla cried out in agony and almost collapsed to the ground from the excruciating pain.

"I like a fiery wench," he commented,

"but I'll teach you who's master!"

He had barely finished the words before he gasped with pain himself, and released his hold on Drusilla so suddenly that she fell to the ground. Half swooning, she lay for a while feeling sick and dizzy from the pain in her arm, and only slowly realised that he had released her. As the mists cleared she thought she could hear the clash of steel upon steel, and harsh breathing. She cautiously opened her eyes, and through the screen of the bushes behind which she was lying saw two figures hotly engaged in a fight.

She could distinguish little, for she was still dizzy, but the taller of the two figures seemed to be gaining the advantage, and was gradually driving the other further away from the bushes. Suddenly Drusilla heard a rustling of the bushes behind her, and turned, fearful of what it might be. To her relief she saw George crawling towards her, a cheeky grin on his face.

"Let's get the horse and go," he whispered. "They'll be too busy fighting over 'ee to notice, and the horse is tethered the far side of the bushes from them."

"Are you badly hurt?" Drusilla asked,

her own senses gradually returning.

"Just winded," he replied. "I managed to wriggle out of the twine, for he's not very good at tying knots!" he whispered with a low chuckle. "Come on!"

She began to crawl after him, and the sounds of the conflict behind them grew fainter. They came to the edge of the bushes and she looked up to see her mare only a few yards away. Unsteadily, she rose to her feet, and took a few faltering steps forwards, at the same time as a scream of agony from behind caused her to turn and almost lose her balance so that she clutched wildly at George who had come to help her.

George peered through the bushes, and reported that one of the men was on the ground.

"He's dead, for sure," he whispered. "The other's sword was right through him. But we'd best be away, lest he wants the horse, too!"

Making what haste she could, Drusilla walked unsteadily across the intervening yards, so short and yet so apparently great a distance, George holding her arm and urging her in a low voice to hurry, as he watched over his shoulder to see what was happening, fearful that the victor of the fight would soon appear to claim the horse.

With a gasp of relief, Drusilla reached the mare and clung to her mane, while the mare, puzzled at these strange doings, nuzzled gently at her shoulder. George was urging Drusilla to put her foot in his cupped hands in order to mount when he suddenly spun round, fists raised, at the sound of a voice behind him.

"There's no haste, lad, I'm here to help you."

Incredulous, Drusilla looked up, and released her hold on the mare, taking a few faltering steps forward.

"Randal! Oh, Randal, thank God!" she gasped, and would have fallen had he not stepped quickly forward to catch her in his arms.

10

"WHAT the devil are you doing here at a time like this?" Randal demanded, in so furious a tone that Drusilla swallowed her tears of relief and drew away from his arms which were supporting her.

"James is hurt!" she explained in a low voice. "He — he was asking for me, and George came to fetch me!"

"And have you so little sense that you attempt to cross a battlefield almost before the battle is concluded, with no more protection than that of a child!"

"I'm nigh on twelve!" George interposed indignantly, but was totally ignored.

"I did not realise it would be — like this!" Drusilla stammered. "But James needed me, and I had to come, whatever the risks!"

"If he sent for you he is a fool!" Randal declared. "He must have been aware of the dangers."

Suddenly Drusilla became angry. She

was still suffering from the pain after the attack on her, and for Randal to be angry with her when they so unexpectedly met again was more than she could bear. She had repeatedly told herself that she would never see him again, that he would marry Mary Percy, and that there was no hope for her, but in her secret dreams she had imagined some enchanted world where the difficulties would be swept away, and he would come to her, Mary Percy no longer mattering to him, and she would discover that he loved her after all. The reality of their meeting, in the aftermath of the battle, with death and violence, blood and anguish all about her, and Randal speaking so harshly, caused her to wrench herself away from him, and speak quickly.

"I do not see what business it is of yours, Sir Randal, that I go to my brother when he is in need! You have no control over my actions! I thank you for intervening and rescuing me from that villain, but I cannot think I shall meet with other such affronts, and so I will bid you farewell. Doubtless you wish to return to your friends!"

His lips twitched, and thinking that he laughed at her, Drusilla flung up her head and walked as steadily as her still shaking legs could carry her across to where her horse was waiting.

"Then I will escort you," Randal said, ignoring her remarks. "Where is your brother?"

"I need no more escort than George!" Drusilla returned, furious with herself for being unable to control her trembling.

"George shall ride your horse and lead the way," Randal said firmly, and before Drusilla realised what he was about he had seized her round the waist and flung her up on to the pommel of his own saddle. Before she recovered her breath he had swung himself up behind her and was holding her in a firm grip.

George, his mouth agape, was uncertain whether to plunge to Drusilla's aid or not, but as the tall man seemed to be known to Drusilla, and did not appear to offer any immediate threats to her safety, he merely watched and waited.

"Where is Mr Matthews?" Randal asked him curtly.

"In our cottage, yonder," George gulped,

pointing along the bottom of the slopes.

"Good, then mount Mistress Drusilla's horse and lead me there," he was ordered, and hastened to obey.

Drusilla remained silent after a brief moment of resistance, when Randal's arm had tightened uncomfortably about her. She knew, when her anger cooled, that she should not have ridden alone, and she was thankful for the security of Randal's protection. Besides, she secretly admitted to herself, there was a bitter sweet emotion in being so close to her beloved, even when he did not love her and held her angrily.

George picked his way along the foot of the hills, and Drusilla looked in horror at the scene of destruction. Men and horses lay sprawled over the slopes, many dead, others suffering from broken limbs. Already Royalist troopers were moving amongst the carnage, putting injured horses out of their misery, taking prisoner and helping away the wounded Roundheads, and leaving until later the men who could not be helped. She assumed it was work of that nature which had brought Randal to the spot, but did not dare to ask him, he looked so stern and forbidding when she glanced through her lashes at him.

They rounded the main bulge of the hills, and began to climb up the more gentle slopes, cutting across the base of the hill until George turned his horse into a trackway leading gradually upwards to the downs. This was an old sheep road, and far easier to negotiate for man and beast than the more precipitous slopes they had passed. After another mile or so George turned off the main track and led them along a scarcely visible path down into a sheltered hollow where the old cottage, which had stood for many generations, hid amongst a tangle of stunted trees and dense bushes.

They halted and George called a greeting which brought Tom to the door. He looked enquiringly at Randal, and then turned to nod to Drusilla.

"Go in to him. I will wait here to escort you home, or otherwise assist you," Randal said abruptly, the first words he had spoken since lifting Drusilla on to his horse. "You need not inform your brother I am here, for fear he thinks I intend to take him for ransom. None shall hear of his presence from me."

Drusilla looked at him quickly, and contrived a tremulous smile, then she slipped down to the ground and followed Tom into the dark interior of the cottage.

As her eyes grew accustomed to the semi-darkness, she saw James lying in a corner on a pile of straw which was covered with a couple of fleeces. His eyes were closed and his face taut with pain, and he had thrown off the rough blanket which had been over him. His leg was strapped to a long straight branch, and his head bound with blood stained rags. Tom crossed to the rough couch and beckoned, smiling reassuringly.

"He is weak, Mistress Drusilla, but will soon recover."

James opened his eyes wide at these words, and looked across at his sister. Drusilla, forgetting all their disagreements, ran to kneel beside him and take his hand in hers.

"Poor James, but thank heaven Tom found you! He knows what to do!"

"I have set the bone, Mistress, but methinks 'twere best to get Mr James home as soon as can be arranged, for I cannot give him the nursing he needs," Tom said quietly.

"Of course he cannot be left here to incommode you!" Drusilla said swiftly. "I will make arrangements as soon as I may. Why did you not send for my father? He could have done this at once."

"I wished to see you — Jacob wanted it, but it was too late!"

"Jacob?" Drusilla asked, peering about her in some anxiety. "James, what is this? Is he here? Is this some ruse?"

"The other man was called Jacob," Tom explained quietly.

"Everyone fled," James said with a groan. "It was shameful! Runaway Hill, it will be called! I tried to ride down by the old sheep road, knowing the rest of the hillside too steep, and Blagrave was with me. He had met the army and decided to stay with us and fight, instead of attempting to return to Reading. It was odd, his wishing to leave Devizes at precisely that time, and I did not rightly understand his explanation," James said with a frown.

"Never mind that," Drusilla said softly,

thinking to herself that Mr Blagrave must have felt intensely chagrined at having fallen in with Waller and been forced to partake in the fighting. "What then happened?"

"Some of Hazelrig's Lobsters came pelting down after us, mad with terror, and taking no care, so that when one of the devils lost his footing we all rolled down in a heap. I was fortunate, for I was in the front and thrown clear, but Blagrave was crushed as they rolled over him. They had such heavy armour, you see, they could scarce move," he explained.

"Yes, so I have been told," Drusilla nodded. "Where is he?"

"We lay there for some time, unable to move, and by great good fortune Tom found us. He brought me here, but when he returned for Blagrave it was too late."

"He was too badly wounded, Mistress, and bled inside," Tom said gently. "Your brother wished us to bring his friend here first, but I could see it would not serve, and indeed he was dead when I went again."

"I — I am sorry for him," Drusilla

said, unable to feel any emotion other than horror at the manner of his death, but James shook his head swiftly.

"He — he may have deserved it!" he jerked out. "Drusilla, I have been so wrong! He confessed to me when we lay there and it seemed we both would die."

"Confessed? What did he have to confess?" she asked, puzzled.

"I'll prepare some broth," Tom said, discreetly moving away to busy himself over a cauldron simmering above the fire at the far side of the room.

"That tale he told me, that Sir Randal Thornton had hired men to attack Elizabeth, was untrue."

"Of course it was!" she said indignantly. "Randal — Sir Randal would not behave so despicably!"

"For you that might have been as difficult to believe as the truth is for me!" he exclaimed. "I could not have credited it had Blagrave not told me himself!"

"What did he tell you?"

James sighed, and seemed unwilling to meet Drusilla's eye.

"It was indefensible," he said slowly, "but I believe the man was desperate. You are too beautiful, my dear, and should have been safely wed long ago!"

"What do you mean?"

"Blagrave was enamoured of you, and terrified that he would lose you to Sir Randal. He confessed that he hired the men to attack Sir Randal and kill him. It was never his intention to involve Elizabeth, but he had told the men they might meet with Sir Randal at my house, and they attacked him straight away instead of following him as had been their orders."

Drusilla was staring at him in horror.

"He intended Sir Randal's death? Oh, how monstrous! And then to accuse Sir Randal of such a plan? I had not thought him so evil!"

James sighed.

"As you know, Elizabeth and I were wed by arrangement, although I came to love her deeply afterwards, so much so that I was near crazed at the loss of her, so I can understand a little of what he felt!"

"But I had given him clearly to

understand that I would never wed him!" Drusilla protested. "It was nought to do with Sir Randal!"

"Blagrave thought that with him disposed of you would turn back to him, for he told me that before Sir Randal appeared you were beginning to favour his suit."

"I never did so! He deluded himself." A sudden thought struck her. "Did he follow us to Thornton Hall and attempt to murder Randal again, when we were riding home?"

"Yes. He guessed where Sir Randal had taken you and followed to Thornton Hall, then again when you set off for home. He told me that he was himself there, but remained hidden, intending to intervene only if it seemed that the other men could not do the business."

"So it was Jacob Blagrave who shot me!" Drusilla exclaimed.

"I am afraid you have much to forgive me," James apologised.

"You? For believing that he was honest? How could you have known?"

"No, not that," James said quickly. "It was our accusations that drove Sir Randal away, that made you refuse him. I cannot

258

tell whether he offered for you merely from a sense of honour. It appears from what I have heard from Blagrave, and the fact that he did court considerable danger himself when he took you from Reading, that he might have had some regard for you. In either event I have done you a great wrong, my dear, and when I am better I intend to seek out Sir Randal and attempt to right matters."

Drusilla was shaking her head in some distress, and both were so deeply absorbed that they did not see George slip into the cottage. He had recovered from his resentment at being called a child, and had been admiring Randal's horse and asking shy questions. A sudden realisation that visitors should be offered some hospitality had sent him scurrying into the cottage, and before Drusilla could decide how best to try and dissuade James from the actions he contemplated, George spoke.

"Tom, shall I take Sir Randal some ale?" he asked, and James twisted to look at him so sharply that he emitted a gasp of pain as he moved his leg.

"Sir Randal? Here?" he demanded.

"Yes, but he intends you no harm!"

Drusilla hastened to assure him.

"Harm? I do not understand. How does he come to be here?"

"He was searching for prisoners," Drusilla explained quickly. "He — we met as I came with George, and he — insisted on coming with me, but he said that he did not propose to hold you to ransom!"

"Then I can speak with him now, and explain. Ransom?" James suddenly asked. "Why ransom? Oh, the battle! I had almost forgot, thinking of this!"

"No, no, that is unimportant! Of course he would not!"

"George, ask Sir Randal to be good enough to speak with me," James went on, ignoring Drusilla's protests, and before she could prevent him George had bounded outside, and a few moments later Sir Randal appeared in the doorway.

He looked across at Drusilla and James, before taking the tankard of ale George poured out for him, then walked across to seat himself on a stool beside James.

"I trust the injury is not too great," he said easily.

"A simple, clean break," Tom assured

him, "and a cut on the head that will soon heal with care."

He looked from one to the other, and making an excuse about needing more wood for the fire, took a reluctant George outside the cottage.

"I have wished to express my regrets for your wife's death," Randal said quietly to James. "I shall ever be remorseful for my part in it, although it was not as Mr Blagrave said. It was because I visited the house, and was forced back into it by the ruffians that set upon me, so I am in part responsible."

"No, no. Blagrave confessed to me that he hired the men to kill you," James said hastily. "I have just been explaining to Drusilla, also that he made another attempt as you were bringing Drusilla home, and it was he that shot her."

"I suspected something of the sort," Randal said, nodding, "but did not wish to accuse him until I had proof, and I have been kept so busy with Prince Maurice in the west that I have had no time to search for that!" he added ruefully. "Where is he?"

"Dead. He was with me, but fatally

injured by the fall that broke my leg. He told me before he died. I was telling Drusilla, never dreaming that you were but outside, that I must see you."

"But you have no need, James, for all is now explained," Drusilla intervened hurriedly. "If Sir Randal will be so good as to escort me, methinks I ought to go back to Devizes and arrange for you to be fetched home."

"There is time for that. I believe, Sir Randal, that the accusations made by Blagrave caused you to leave Devizes after you had offered for my sister. Drusilla may have been swayed by them — "

"No, I never believed that of him, never!" Drusilla cried in distress.

"Then why did you refuse Sir Randal's offer, my love?" James asked, puzzled.

"I have told you!" Driven into making an explanation, Drusilla dared not look at Sir Randal, and did not see the arrested expression on his face. She spoke so quietly that the two men had difficulty in hearing her, and James asked her to repeat what she had said.

"Sir Randal does not truly wish to marry me!" she said curtly.

Randal surveyed her calmly for a moment, and then rose to his feet.

"If you will excuse us, Mr Matthews, I think it would be best if we followed your sister's suggestion and sought help to move you. We can discuss this matter on the way."

Not permitting a surprised and rather bewildered James time to reply, he bowed, smiled, and took Drusilla's arm in a firm grasp, leading her from the cottage before she had time to protest.

The horses were tethered nearby, and sound of wood being chopped indicated the whereabouts of Tom and George. Randal, drawing Drusilla irresistibly along with him, walked past the horses to a small grassy patch of ground sheltered from the winds by some fruit trees, and facing the setting sun. He halted, pulling Drusilla round to face him, and when she resolutely refrained from looking at him, pulled her chin gently to turn her face up to his.

"When I offered for you, Drusilla my sweet, did you imagine that I did it unwillingly, that I felt obliged to do so because of the accident that we had been so long alone together?"

"No, I knew that was not important, as I told you!" she said. "My father did not understand!"

"He thought I had made the offer because of that?"

"That is what he told me," she answered at last.

"And you refused me because you did not wish for an unwilling husband?"

"No! Not because of that!"

"Well, my dearest, I never thought that you believed those lies of Blagrave, so what reason have you for saying I do not wish to marry you? Is it some strange way of saying that you do not wish to marry me?"

She did not answer, for she could neither agree with nor deny his suggestion, and he slipped his arms about her and drew her close to him.

"My lovely one, I am older than you, and have been about the world a great deal, and observed people more than you have been able to. I prided myself that I knew when a woman loved a man, that I could distinguish looks of love from those of coquetry or mere liking. When I saw you I knew that there would never be any other woman for me, and I thought you came to feel love for me. Was I so completely mistaken?"

Wordlessly, Drusilla shook her head, and Randal's arms tightened suffocatingly about her.

"Then why did you refuse me?"

There was nothing for it except to tell the truth, and Drusilla took a deep breath and spoke, still avoiding looking at him.

"It was because of Mary Percy!" she exclaimed.

"Mary?" There was genuine puzzlement in Randal's voice, so that Drusilla, startled, risked a glance at him. "What has Mary Percy to do with us?"

"I thought that you intended — wanted — to marry her! I had heard, from Mistress Rogers, that you were paying her many attentions in Oxford, and then, your sister and Barbara seemed to be so sure of it, and Mary herself — she behaved as though she was certain of becoming your wife!"

Randal gave a soft chuckle.

"My foolish little love! You know so little of the world! Yes, I admit I paid her attentions, but no more than I have for years paid attentions to pretty women that I had no wish to marry! My sister, I can well believe, would busy herself spreading rumours, for she has long despaired of marrying me off, and hoped that Mary, with her wealth and beauty, might tempt me. Mary may have thought so, too, and if so I am sorry, but I have never given her cause to do so. I do not need wealth, and you have more beauty than a dozen Mary Percy's!"

Unwilling to permit herself to believe what he was saying, Drusilla was staring up into his eyes, and at these last words she disbelievingly shook her head.

"Oh, but she is lovely!" she could not help exclaiming, and he laughed.

"Yes, mayhap, but I prefer your style of beauty! Besides, you have so much more to give me, and I love you, and I did not love Mary! Was that the barrier you thought lay between us?"

"You cannot possibly prefer me!" she whispered, and he bent down to kiss her, gently at first, but with a growing passion so that Drusilla, finally accepting the truth, the incredible reality of his words, responded blissfully.

When he finally released her she could not speak, but looked up at him wonderingly, and he tenderly took her hands and kissed them, looking all the while deep into her eyes.

"Drusilla, my dearest, lovely Drusilla, will you marry me?"

"I — oh yes, Randal! I have been so unhappy since you went away!"

He clasped her tightly in his arms again.

"I never want you to be unhappy again! Will you marry me immediately? Do you think your parents will agree? I did not obtain the impression that your father was against my suit!"

Drusilla chuckled.

"Oh, no, he was most impressed by your title!" She sighed a little. "He has always had great ambitions for his children. Even when he half-believed that you might have hired those men, he was prepared to overlook it for the sake of that! Why, he even believed that I had exaggerated the injury to my head to compromise you!" she recalled. "I truly think that supposed aspect of my behaviour pleased him more than anything else I have ever done, for he thought it very intelligent of me! He said I would have been clever at business!"

Randal laughed.

"Then we had best return and inform him that you are going to be Lady Thornton! When we have fetched James to Devizes we will make our own arrangements, and as soon as we are wed I will take you to Thornton Hall."

"Your sister!" Drusilla exclaimed. "She will be far from pleased! I do not think she liked me? Will she still be there?"

"She may be disappointed that her own schemes have failed, but she will be happy to see me wed. Besides, I have never criticised her choice of husbands, and she will say no word against you, for if she does she will never visit us again! She is to be married herself in a few days, and I will ensure that she leaves Thornton Hall before I take you there, for I know she can be intimidating. It is your home, my love, to do with as you wish, and I know that with you it will be a real home, the one I have dreamed of, and I still cannot believe my good fortune in having found you!"

"You were so angry when you found me tonight," she recalled.

"Not with you. Never with you, my love. I was appalled at the danger you ran, but I realise now that, never having seen a battle, you could not have known what it would be like, with desperate men searching for escape or for loot."

Drusilla shuddered.

"I heard, in the town, that you won despite the numbers against you."

"Waller had twice our number of horse, and the foot also. It was a tremendous victory. But there would have been no joy in it for me if I had not won you."

They realised some time later that the sun had almost slipped over the horizon, and Randal somewhat guiltily laughed, saying that he would have to make reparation to Tom and George if they had been chopping wood unnecessarily all the time.

"And James will feel neglected if they are not with him. Come, we must ride home."

But they found when they reached the horses that Tom had returned to the cottage, for the soft glow of a candle was visible through the small window. They rode back to Devizes in the gathering twilight around the edge of 'Runaway Hill', hand in hand, content to forget the struggle that had taken place on it in the blissful contemplation of their own joy.

THE END

THE WILDERNESS WALK
Sheila Bishop

Stifling unpleasant memories of a misbegotten romance in Cleave with Lord Francis Aubrey, Lavinia goes on holiday there with her sister. The two women are thrust into a romantic intrigue involving none other than Lord Francis.

THE RELUCTANT GUEST
Rosalind Brett

Ann Calvert went to spend a month on a South African farm with Theo Borland and his sister. They both proved to be different from her first idea of them, and there was Storr Peterson — the most disturbing man she had ever met.

ONE ENCHANTED SUMMER
Anne Tedlock Brooks

A tale of mystery and romance and a girl who found both during one enchanted summer.

CLOUD OVER MALVERTON
Nancy Buckingham

Dulcie soon realises that something is seriously wrong at Malverton, and when violence strikes she is horrified to find herself under suspicion of murder.

AFTER THOUGHTS
Max Bygraves

The Cockney entertainer tells stories of his East End childhood, of his RAF days, and his post-war showbusiness successes and friendships with fellow comedians.

MOONLIGHT AND MARCH ROSES
D. Y. Cameron

Lynn's search to trace a missing girl takes her to Spain, where she meets Clive Hendon. While untangling the situation, she untangles her emotions and decides on her own future.

TIGER TIGER
Frank Ryan

A young man involved in drugs is found murdered. This is the first event which will draw Detective Inspector Sandy Woodings into a whirlpool of murder and deceit.

CAROLINE MINUSCULE
Andrew Taylor

Caroline Minuscule, a medieval script, is the first clue to the whereabouts of a cache of diamonds. The search becomes a deadly kind of fairy story in which several murders have an other-worldly quality.

LONG CHAIN OF DEATH
Sarah Wolf

During the Second World War four American teenagers from the same town join the Army together. Forty-two years later, the son of one of the soldiers realises that someone is systematically wiping out the families of the four men.

BUTTERFLY MONTANE
Dorothy Cork

Parma had come to New Guinea to marry Alec Rivers, but she found him completely disinterested and that overbearing Pierce Adams getting entirely the wrong idea about her.

HONOURABLE FRIENDS
Janet Daley

Priscilla Burford is happily married when she meets Junior Environment Minister Alistair Thurston. Inevitably, sexual obsession and political necessity collide.

WANDERING MINSTRELS
Mary Delorme

Stella Wade's career as a concert pianist might have been ruined by the rudeness of a famous conductor, so it seemed to her agent and benefactor. Even Sir Nicholas fails to see the possibilities when John Tallis falls deeply in love with Stella.

A GREAT DELIVERANCE
Elizabeth George

Into the web of old houses and secrets of Keldale Valley comes Scotland Yard Inspector Thomas Lynley and his assistant to solve a particularly savage murder.

'E' IS FOR EVIDENCE
Sue Grafton

Kinsey Millhone was bogged down on a warehouse fire claim. It came as something of a shock when she was accused of being on the take. She'd been set up. Now she had a new client — herself.

A FAMILY OUTING IN AFRICA
Charles Hampton and Janie Hampton

A tale of a young family's journey through Central Africa by bus, train, river boat, lorry, wooden bicyle and foot.

DEATH TRAIN
Robert Byrne

The tale of a freight train out of control and leaking a paralytic nerve gas that turns America's West into a scene of chemical catastrophe in which whole towns are rendered helpless.

THE ADVENTURE
OF THE
CHRISTMAS PUDDING
Agatha Christie

In the introduction to this short story collection the author wrote "This book of Christmas fare may be described as 'The Chef's Selection'. I am the Chef!"

RETURN TO BALANDRA
Grace Driver

Returning to her Caribbean island home, Suzanne looks forward to being with her parents again, but most of all she longs to see Wim van Branden, a coffee planter she has known all her life.

BALLET GENIUS
Gillian Freeman and Edward Thorpe

Presents twenty pen portraits of great dancers of the twentieth century and gives an insight into their daily lives, their professional careers, the ever present risk of injury and the pressure to stay on top.

TO LIVE IN PEACE
Rosemary Friedman

The final part of the author's Anglo-Jewish trilogy, which began with PROOFS OF AFFECTION and ROSE OF JERICHO, telling the story of Kitty Shelton, widowed after a happy marriage, and her three children.

NORA WAS A NURSE
Peggy Gaddis

Nurse Nora Courtney was hopelessly in love with Doctor Owen Baird and when beautiful Lillian Halstead set her cap for him, Nora realised she must make him see her as a desirable woman as well as an efficient nurse.

IN PALE BATTALIONS
Robert Goddard

Leonora Galloway has waited all her life to learn the truth about her father, slain on the Somme before she was born, the truth about the death of her mother and the mystery of an unsolved wartime murder.

A DREAM FOR TOMORROW
Grace Goodwin

In her new position as resident nurse at Coombe Magna, Karen Stevens has to bear the emnity of the beautiful Lisa, secretary to the doctor-on-call.

AFTER EMMA
Sheila Hocken

Following the author's previous auto-biographies — EMMA & I, and EMMA & Co., she relates more of the hilarious (and sometimes despairing) antics of her guide dogs.

THE SONG OF THE PINES
Christina Green

Taken to a Greek island as substitute for David Nicholas's secretary, Annie quickly falls prey to the island's charms and to the charms of both Marcus, the Greek, and David himself.

GOODBYE DOCTOR GARLAND
Marjorie Harte

The story of a woman doctor who gave too much to her profession and almost lost her personal happiness.

DIGBY
Pamela Hill

Welcomed at courts throughout Europe, Kenelm Digby was the particular favourite of the Queen of France, who wanted him to be her lover, but the beautiful Venetia was the mainspring of his life.

DEATH ON A HOT SUMMER NIGHT
Anne Infante

Micky Douglas is either accident-prone or someone is trying to kill him. He finds himself caught in a desperate race to save his ex-wife and others from a ruthless gang.

HOLD DOWN A SHADOW
Geoffrey Jenkins

Maluti Rider, with the help of four of the world's most wanted men, is determined to destroy the Katse Dam and release a killer flood.

THAT NICE MISS SMITH
Nigel Morland

A reconstruction and reassessment of the trial in 1857 of Madeleine Smith, who was acquitted by a verdict of Not Proven of poisoning her lover, Emile L'Angelier.

CHATEAU OF FLOWERS
Margaret Rome

Alain, Comte de Treville needed a wife to look after him, and Fleur went into marriage on a business basis only, hoping that eventually he would come to trust and care for her.

CRISS-CROSS
Alan Scholefield

As her ex-husband had succeeded in kidnapping their young daughter once, Jane was determined to take her safely back to England. But all too soon Jane is caught up in a new web of intrigue.

DEAD BY MORNING
Dorothy Simpson

Leo Martindale's body was discovered outside the gates of his ancestral home. Is it, as Inspector Thanet begins to suspect, murder?